TERESA'S DECISION

by the same author

fiction

Natana, a novel
Kintalloch, a novel

translation

Weir de Hermiston i altres relats
(R. L. Stevenson's *Weir of Hermiston* in Catalan)

Teresa's Decision

Tales of Catalonia & Scotland
Past & Present
With a Foreword by Medardo Fraile

Mercedes Clarasó

BLACK ACE BOOKS

First published in 1995 by
Black Ace Books, Ellemford, Duns
Berwickshire, TD11 3SG, Scotland

© Mercedes Clarasó 1995
Foreword © Medardo Fraile 1995

Typeset in Scotland by Black Ace Editorial

Printed in Great Britain by Antony Rowe Ltd
Bumper's Farm, Chippenham, SN14 6QA

A CIP catalogue record for this book
is available from the British Library

ISBN   1-872988-36-9

The publishers gratefully acknowledge
subsidy from the Scottish Arts Council
towards the production of this volume

ACKNOWLEDGEMENTS

'Fey' won third prize in the 1993 Bridport Creative Writing Competition and was first published in 1993 in *The Bridport Prize*, published by Redcliffe Press Ltd, Bristol, for Bridport Arts Centre, South Street, Bridport, Dorset.

'The Wall' was first published in *The Devil and Dr Tuberose*, the HarperCollins / Scottish Arts Council annual anthology of short stories for 1991.

The author and publishers gratefully acknowledge that the story entitled 'The Wee Malkie' was suggested by Stephen Mulrine's poem 'The Coming of the Wee Malkies'.

In memory of my mother and father
whose Scottish and Catalan roots live on
in some of these stories

CONTENTS

Foreword

In a Hispanists' conference which took place in Cardiff about nineteen years ago I saw in the audience a slim woman with a fringe, who looked rather like Carson McCullers, the unforgettable author of *The Ballad of the Sad Café* and *The Heart is a Lonely Hunter*, among other memorable stories. I sat down next to her and it turned out that she spoke my language very well and, into the bargain, she knew my reputation as a writer. She was teaching in the University of St Andrews and lived in Cupar, which was within reach of Glasgow, where I lived.

After the conference she invited me to give a talk to her students, which I did on several occasions. And so I got to know her house in Cupar, where she lived with her cats, and with which I literally fell in love. That house, long and deep like a cargo ship, with a little bridge passing over a lane, taking you into a yard which Mercedes had converted into a garden full of flowers and vegetables, was the perfect setting for an excellent novel of intrigue. But what was remarkable was not only the choice of the house but also its décor, achieved with few elements, but all of them creative, striking, arranged with a confident courage which reminded me of the achievements of popular Catalan art, so highly valued by great artists, including Picasso, from the cultural movement of the Catalan renaissance of the last century right up to the present day. In the interior of that house I saw a swarm of possibilities, as I also saw, later, in a cottage which Mercedes rented in Nydie Mains, and now in her house in Oxton.

One writer recognizes another, even when disguised as a lecturer who has not yet written or published a single line of fiction, among other reasons because the writer thinks about others and thinks again, since people are the very stuff he works with.

Mercedes was, in the best sense of the word, a rarity, an attractive rarity, because of her birth – half Catalan, half Scot – and because of other circumstances in her childhood and her life; she lived surrounded by books, music, colours, magic – all kinds of languages, as it were, suggestions and signs – and she seemed to scrutinize every inch of her house with the same attention as someone who looks at, reads or corrects a page he has just written. The attitude which she attributes to the protagonist of one of her most striking stories, 'The Wall', could in part be her own:

'She wanted to become the place itself, just as the dry and dusty road was the place, and the dark green forest beyond was also the place. She wanted to assume the consciousness of this piece of soil that she had known and served all her life.'

Mercedes was, besides, a solitary person, with a wild taste for roaming in the hills, and therefore good at listening – to people and nature – and obviously never lonely. She also had a good memory. This, of course, is not essential for writing, because memories can be just as easily invented as faithfully reproduced. I was never aware that she wrote poetry, but I was always sure that she *could* write poetry or anything else, and I on several occasions encouraged her to start writing. One day she heeded me, and she heeded herself, and she started sending the stories she was writing, for me to read.

'The Wall', an outstanding story in a Latin American setting, was published immediately in an anthology of Scottish Short Stories in 1991; it is in my opinion the best story in that book. In 1993 and 1994 two of her novels came out, *Natana*, short-listed for the Authors' Club Best First Novel Award of 1994, and *Kintalloch, a Tale of Scottish Family Life*. In both of these, as in six of the stories which the reader will meet in this volume, memories of Catalonia during the Civil War and post-war years, and of its literature, appear from time to time in their pages, where Scottish and Spanish elements alternate as in the life of the author herself, who spent years of her childhood and youth in the little town of Masnou, near Barcelona, and also in Valencia. Two wars have shaken her life and left their mark on her prose; the Spanish Civil War and the Second World War, both of which she spent in Glasgow and then in Dumfriesshire with her mother and sister, separated from don José, her father, for eleven years.

These stories constitute another upward step towards Mercedes Clarasó's definitive presence in literature, because, contrary to the opinions of those who don't quite manage to understand this genre, I insist that no poet, novelist or dramatist should be considered a fully-fledged writer until he or she has succeeded in writing a good short story, which is the unalloyed quintessence of all the qualities found in the best writers. Mercedes Clarasó is a novelist and she is also a writer. Stories such as the one already mentioned, or 'Just Waiting', 'Fey', 'The Song of the Rising Sap', 'Hard Folk', 'Under the Stairs', 'Riders', 'Golden Means', 'Wild Wattie', or 'The Thimble', and others, will undoubtedly convince the most recalcitrant reader and will delight the true connoisseur of the short story.

Medardo Fraile
January 1995

1

Teresa's Decision

'I'm not going a step further,' the woman announced suddenly.

'Come on, we've no time to stop for rests.' Without turning to look at his wife, the man flung the words back in her direction.

'I'm not resting. I'm just not going on.' Teresa had stopped beside one of the few trees at the side of the road. It was an old, twisted olive tree, and she half stood, half sat, supported by a bend in its trunk.

The man stopped and looked at her across the ten or twelve yards that now separated them.

'You *are* resting,' he pointed out. 'You know the troops are advancing. We've got to get to the frontier before they catch up with us.'

Teresa thought of the seemingly endless miles they had already travelled since they set out two days ago, and then she thought of the days, if not weeks, it would take them to reach the border. 'The frontier!' she snorted. 'That'll be the day!'

Slowly and angrily Gabriel retraced his steps and stood in front of his wife.

'You know what will happen if they get me, don't you?'

'We'll never make it to the frontier. Never. I'm done in already. I'm going back home.'

'You're mad. You know I can't go back.'

'Don't, then. I'm not asking you to.' Her voice had

uttered the words, but she could hardly believe the enormity of what she was saying.

For a moment the man's face registered nothing but incredulity. Then he looked up from the dusty road on which his eyes had been fixed, and Teresa saw a gleam of something in them that she couldn't quite interpret.

'You mean you want me to go on alone?' he asked.

For a while they argued about what they should do. Teresa began to suspect that he was perhaps even more keen to go on without her than with her. But it was difficult for him to agree to going off and leaving her alone and unprotected in a war-torn country, miles from home. She was convinced they wanted the same thing, but neither had the courage to put it into words.

At last she found the saving formula. 'I'll try to get a lift with some family, or in one of the lorries. Then we can meet up further on.'

'Yes,' he said, 'yes, that's it. I'll look out for you, and we'll meet up further on. That will be the best way.'

They both knew how improbable this was. The cars and lorries that had passed them had all been heavily loaded, and their occupants had driven past with at most a sad wave of the hand as an acknowledgement of their shared misfortune. As a feasible plan of campaign the suggestion was almost valueless, but it served its purpose.

'Well, you'd better get on,' she prompted.

'Yes, I'd better go. Well then . . . ' He hesitated. As they hadn't admitted the probable finality of their parting, farewells seemed out of place. 'Well, I'll see you later,' he said abruptly, and began the long journey again.

Teresa watched him, and noticed that he walked more lightly, as if delivered of a burden. Her eyes followed him till he disappeared from sight. Not once did he turn back to look or wave.

For a long time she rested against the tree, trying to take in what had happened. After forty years of marriage, here she was, suddenly on her own, with no likelihood of ever seeing her husband again, for she had no intention of following him to the frontier, and she was sure he had understood this. It was an astounding fact, the more so in that it had come so suddenly, so effortlessly. For forty years she had been tied to this man and never, in spite of her unhappiness, had it occurred to her that anything short of death could separate them. Now it had happened, and she didn't know how or why. It was just one of the astonishing things that the Civil War had brought. Two days ago, just before leaving home, she had never thought they would flee at a moment's notice. She never thought she would walk past an unburied corpse on the roadside, without even stopping to say a hurried, horrified prayer.

But the war had brought these things, and what most amazed her was the simplicity with which she had accepted them, as if they were the most natural thing in the world. And now this – the end of her marriage, without tears or reproaches or recriminations. Above all, with no previous intention on either side of ending the troublesome yoke. She tried to discover what part of her had refused to go on. She was quite unaware of having had any such intention. And why today, and not yesterday, or tomorrow? And why in that particular place? It was as if the old tree had beckoned to her, telling her that this was where she could lay down her burden.

And that was, in effect, the most powerful of all the sensations she felt, the consciousness that she could now rest. Forty years, she thought, forty years of grinding work, of always knowing there was something else to be done, in the house, in the fields, looking after the children. Working from dawn to long past dusk. And not much rest at night either, till Gabriel was satisfied. Only during the last few years had she had peace at night, with no crying children and no demands from her husband.

After Gabriel had disappeared from view she settled herself more comfortably against the tree, and looked about her with a rare, voluptuous sense of leisure. She decided she would spend some time simply resting, luxuriating in her idleness, living only in the present, this wonderful moment of ungrudged rest.

Like a lady, she thought, like a city lady, out for her *paseo* in the park, having a rest on one of the stone seats in the shade. Only there it would be the shade of a mimosa or a magnolia, or something fancy like that, not an old olive tree. For a while she roamed in her imaginary park, with its fountains and flower beds, listening to bird song, watching well dressed children as they chased each other along the paths. She had often passed such a park on her way to the market in Valencia to sell her vegetables. But she had never had the time to stop and enjoy its peace and quiet. Always something else to do, she thought, that's what my life has been, one long effort to find enough time to do all that has to be done. And now, now it's all changed, and I don't even know why.

Her eyes wandered over the arid scene in front of her and she began to feel that perhaps the change of scenery was responsible for what had happened. For the first day of their flight they had been travelling through the familiar backcloth of the Valencian *huerta*, with its flat, well tended expanse of green – the green of the young rice in its season, the green of the vegetables she had spent her life growing and selling. It was a peaceful, fruitful, well watered landscape.

And it was the only one she knew.

But then the scene had changed. As the ground began gradually to rise, the lush green had disappeared, apart from a few isolated patches of vegetables here and there. Now the green had disappeared altogether. The soil was dry and dusty, and most of it seemed to produce nothing but a sparse, maquis-like vegetation. The loss of the fertile plain had filled Teresa with a sense of desolation. Not only was she leaving her own home behind her, but she now found herself in a hostile, barren land, such as she had never seen before.

All day this strange, dried-out landscape had weighed upon her spirit, as if the very soil under her feet had become a symbol of her homelessness and her uprooting. And yet she had not been aware of any protest within her. She was tired, worn out; she was depressed, even despairing about the outcome of their flight; but it had never crossed her mind that she could refuse to go on. She just had to keep walking beside her husband, in spite of her fears and her exhaustion. And then, unannounced, she had heard herself telling Gabriel that she wasn't going on. Even on a less fateful journey, such a statement from her would have been unthinkable.

She had never disobeyed her husband before.

To stop for a rest, even on their way home from the market, would have been inconceivable. The fact that on this occasion she had refused to go any further, thus in effect breaking up their marriage, was hardly more amazing. It must be the war, she thought. Or this hard, cruel landscape. I must get back to the *huerta*. I've surely rested enough now.

With an effort she dragged herself up and stood beside the tree, resting her hand on its ridged trunk. I'll remember this tree, she thought. It's changed my life. She gave the tree a little pat, almost of complicity, stepped out on to the road and started walking back towards the plains. With every step she was adding to the distance between her and her husband. She thought of this, and wondered whether she should feel guilty about it. So far all she could feel was a kind of stunned wonder, and a lightness in her walk that reminded her of Gabriel's step as he walked away from her. As if both of them had cast off a burden.

After a while she began to feel hungry. She stopped and opened up the bundle of stuff she carried with her, all her worldly goods, wrapped up in the traditional checked cotton square. As she took the bread out she realized she had all of Gabriel's rations as well as her own. For the first time she felt a stab of unmistakable guilt. This was rapidly superseded by the shocked realization that Gabriel had all the money. That was the natural way, of course. The woman carried the food, while the man was in charge of the money. And that was fine, as long as they were together. But now . . .

She walked on as she ate her bread, anxious to get back to her own type of country before night. By now she was again very tired, but the ground was getting flatter, green patches were beginning to appear again, and she trudged on in the hope of getting to the last *barraca* they had passed that morning. She remembered looking at it and wondering whether they would see any more, for she realized they were coming to the end of the *huerta*.

Her eyes kept scanning the horizon for this first symbol of her own habitat. If she could only get there before dark she would knock on the door and ask them to let her in for the night. Surely they wouldn't refuse a solitary woman! She hurried on, walking faster than before in spite of her exhaustion. At last, well before sunset, she caught a glimpse of the high, pointed roof, and was soon able to recognize the little cross at the top. The house stood a few yards off the road, on the far side of one of the irrigation ditches. She crossed this by the bridge and followed the path to the house, feasting her eyes on the fresh green of the well watered vegetables.

As she reached the house she became aware of a great silence. She knocked repeatedly, but got no reply. Perhaps the owners had fled. She tried the door handle and found it yielded. Standing in the open doorway she looked into the cool, empty building. The key was in the lock. Did this mean that the owners were somewhere nearby, and might come back any moment? Or had they fled in such haste and despair that they hadn't even thought of locking the door? She found the remains of a meal on the table, and clothes and other objects lying about, and decided that they must have fled.

Well, at least she had a roof over her head for the night. Reflecting that this would be the first time she had ever slept alone in a house, she locked the door and wondered whether she ought to feel nervous. But she was too numbed by the tremendous change that she herself had brought about in her life. Besides, she was too tired to care. She lay down on the bed and fell asleep almost at once.

She woke up to hear knocking on the door and voices outside. It was now completely dark. For the first time she fully realized her position, and terror seized her. Here she was, locked into a strange house, lying on some stranger's bed, miles away from her home, miles away from her husband, with someone outside trying to get in. She lay still, rigid with fear, praying that the strangers would go away.

After another round of knocking and a little more conversation they must have decided to leave, for the voices

21

became fainter. And then she heard a child beginning to cry, and a woman's voice comforting it, growing fainter.

'Wait,' she called out. 'Wait, I'm coming.' She leapt up and stumbled across the floor, still calling out. At last she found the door and opened it. In the starlight she was able to make out the forms of a man and a woman. The woman had a baby in her arms, and the man was carrying two small children, one of them still sobbing gently.

'Poor lamb, poor lamb,' crooned Teresa, as she took the sobbing child from its father's arms and held it close.

The man struck a match and with it they lit a candle they found lying on the table. The strangers had brought some food, and Teresa added some of her store. They sat round the table in the flickering light, eating and talking. The young couple had come from a village some miles south of Teresa's. They too were fleeing before the advance of Franco's troops.

'They will call us reds. God knows what they would do to us,' sighed the woman. 'And yet we've done no harm to anyone.'

'Politics!' exclaimed Teresa. 'I wish the men would leave these things alone.'

'You can't leave injustice alone,' said the man.

'Yes, Manolo, that's all very well,' put in his wife. 'But there was no need for us to interfere. We were all right.'

'*We* were all right. But what about some of the others? What about the poverty and injustice all round about us? A man must speak out. That's what politics is about. It's a way of helping your neighbour.'

Teresa gave a sudden, sardonic laugh. 'Not for my Gabriel, it isn't. It's a way of hating your neighbours. He was always angry, always getting at someone in the name of politics. Talking all the time, talking, talking, venting his anger.'

'God knows,' said the man, 'there are things enough in this world to make you angry. But anger isn't enough.'

'Well, that's all he's got. Just anger, and words, words, words.'

'Is that why you left him?' The couple had listened to her story and, like Teresa herself, been puzzled as to why precisely she had turned back, leaving her husband to go on without her.

Teresa thought the matter over. 'I don't know, I really don't know. Something inside me just said, "That's enough." At first I thought it just meant the walking. But it's changed my whole life. Perhaps that's what it really meant, deep inside.'

'There's odd things go on inside us, right enough,' mused the woman. 'Take my mother, for instance. We've been talking for weeks about getting out if the others got near enough, and my mother was to come with us. It was all settled. And yet, when we left this morning, she refused to come. Said she wanted to be buried beside my father, said she couldn't go away and die in foreign parts. And that was it – daughter, grandchildren, nothing could move her. And yet, she'd agreed she would come with us.'

'I suppose she felt the same as I felt. Something happened inside her that went against all she was meaning to do. I'm glad you told me that. It makes me feel less . . . less odd.'

Teresa had been holding one of the children on her lap as they sat and talked. The little girl had been sleeping, but now she opened her eyes and looked about her, half frightened. Teresa held her close and began to rock her gently again. She watched as the child relaxed and smiled, reassured; then a glazed look settled on the eyes, and the eyelids fluttered once or twice, then lay still against the pale skin, like a fringe of dark lace. Suddenly and intensely Teresa relived the miraculous moments when first her own children, and then her grandchildren, had fallen asleep in her arms. She felt the old sense of oneness with this young flesh resting so trustingly on her body.

The others had started to talk about their plans for the morning.

'You'll come with us,' said the man.

'Oh, no. I can't come with you. I'm going back home.'

In the end they convinced her that, as the wife of a red, she would be in great danger once the nationalists took over. They insisted that she must go with them. There was room in the van, since Carmen's mother had refused to come. Still she demurred. She pointed out that she had nothing to share with them, and couldn't pay her way.

'Well, but you might meet up with your husband again, if you come with us. And if not, if you don't see him, or don't want . . . well, anyway, you could just stay with us.'

'I'd only be a burden. What can I do? What help can I be to you?'

Carmen smiled. 'Just look,' she said, 'just look at that child asleep on your lap. And think what it's like in the van, with Manolo driving, and only me to keep all the children happy. We thought my mother would be there to help. We'll have you instead.'

Teresa felt almost overwhelmed by their kindness, but couldn't decide what to do. She was still undecided when they all settled down for the night. The two women shared the bed, with the three little ones packed in between them, while Manolo slept on the floor.

After the candle had been blown out Teresa spoke.

'It's a terrible thing, war – wicked and horrible and cruel. And yet, there's another side to it. It makes it possible for wonderful things to happen.'

The younger woman answered after a pause. 'Yes, I know

what you mean. I think my children have just found a new grandmother, the very day they lost their old one.'

'Hush, woman, hush,' murmured Teresa, and fell into a peaceful sleep.

The following morning the couple seemed to take it for granted that Teresa was going with them, at least till they met up with her husband. And out of sheer indecision she found herself setting off with them, still with no clear idea in her mind. If they didn't meet up with Gabriel, then there was no problem. She would stay with these kind friends as long as they would have her. But if they came across Gabriel . . .

Perhaps they could once again pretend, and assume that they'd meet later on, once they had crossed the frontier. That would be a way out of the dilemma for both of them. For she had a strong suspicion that Gabriel didn't really want her company any more than she wanted his. But the danger was that he might feel obliged to claim her, especially in the presence of other people. Her only certainty was that she didn't want to get out of the van and start walking with him again. She now knew for sure that she didn't want to spend the rest of her life with him, acting as his drudge, putting up with his bad temper and listening to his endless tirades. But she also suspected that she would obey if he commanded her to stay with him. And if that happened, then the past few hours, with their tantalizing taste of rest and freedom, would become nothing more than an unaccountable parenthesis in her life.

As they journeyed she kept recognizing the places she had passed the previous day. Strangely, though they soon left her beloved *huerta* well behind, this arid landscape no longer looked as hostile as before. Perhaps because it had already become slightly familiar – she was seeing this stretch of road for the third time now. Perhaps because she was travelling in comfort now, instead of walking. And perhaps because she was now in congenial company.

But the moment they came to the tree where she and her husband had parted, she began to feel nervous. She would have liked to ask them to stop, to let her spend a little time beside the tree, and to touch its rough bark. But she said nothing, keeping her eyes on the road, even though she knew that Gabriel must have travelled many miles further by now. Occasionally they passed other travellers, some alone, some in twos or threes, some crowded into a cart or *tartana* drawn by a tired horse. Teresa examined each solitary figure as it appeared, holding her breath. Perhaps if she saw him in time she could pretend she had dropped something and grope about on the floor of the van till she was out of danger of being recognized. After all, Gabriel would be looking out for her, and this seemed the only way to escape his notice.

When at last he came in sight she didn't realize who it was till they were nearly level with him, for she had been looking for a solitary figure, and now he had a companion. Another man was walking beside him, and the two were talking eagerly. Or rather, it was Gabriel who was doing the talking. She could see that from his excited, angry gestures. She expected him to turn round at the sound of the approaching vehicle and examine its passengers in search of his wife. But as they overtook him he still hadn't turned round to look at the van. In spite of her fear of being recognized she couldn't resist the temptation to look back and see how he reacted. Gabriel strode on, gesticulating. Either he was too engrossed in his subject to notice the van, or he was taking good care not to look at it. Or perhaps he had forgotten by now that he'd ever had a wife.

* * *

26

Early in the afternoon Manolo remarked on the fact that they hadn't caught up with Teresa's husband. 'Perhaps he's got a lift,' he suggested.

'No, he hasn't. He's still walking.'

'How do you know?'

'We passed him two hours ago. He never looked up.'

'And you said nothing?'

'And I said nothing.' She spoke the words solemnly, with just a touch of pride.

As they crossed the frontier she reflected that she had never been so free in her life, for she had nothing to lose. Her children had all grown up and gone from her, she had lost her home and her homeland, and she had willingly accepted the fact that circumstances had connived at separating her from her husband. She felt that, whatever hardships had to be faced, she was in a good position to face them.

And hardships there were, even though she and her adopted family were among the lucky ones, for Manolo had a brother working in Toulouse. At first they stayed with him, and Teresa looked after the little ones while their parents went in search of work. It was a long, hard struggle, but ultimately they got jobs, found a flat and settled down. Teresa had fallen into the role of grandmother, in charge of the children, cooking and housework. She even learned enough market French to be able to do the shopping. She tried not to think of the future, and neither Carmen nor Manolo ever referred to it. The children, of course, took it for granted that she was a permanent feature of their lives, and she herself could see nothing else in the future. Nor did she ask for anything else. As the family's standard of living rose, Teresa found life easier and pleasanter than it had ever been.

Sometimes she thought of Gabriel and wondered what had become of him. And often she thought of her beloved *huerta*, but with affection rather than active nostalgia. After the first few months she began to get letters from her sister Ramona and from the more verbally gifted of her children. Life at home seemed to be very hard indeed, with poverty more grinding than ever, and repression at its fiercest, from what she could read between the lines. If they had stayed, Gabriel's reputation would have made life impossible for them, perhaps literally.

Then, after they had been in France for ten years, Teresa received a letter from her sister, a much longer letter than usual, with the news that Ramona's husband had died, and that she wanted Teresa to come and live with her. The couple had been childless, and Ramona felt very lonely living alone. She assured Teresa that she need have no fear of reprisals if she came without her troublemaking husband.

Teresa felt doubtful. Even after the lapse of ten years, word was still coming back from Spain of exiles who had returned and immediately been put in prison. Others had disappeared. Others found it impossible to get work. The Civil War had not been forgotten. One could hardly even say that it was over. But after all, she thought, I'm an old woman. Why should they bother about me? But the thought of leaving her new family, especially the children, filled her with sadness. She sat thinking about the letter for a long time, reluctant to give up her present contented life.

And then, suddenly, she saw the *huerta*. With startling clarity the picture appeared before her eyes, and all the repressed longing of the last ten years seemed to explode inside her. The green and gentle landscape appeared to her as the purest symbol of order and plenty and, above all, peace. Manolo and Carmen had taken her to see some of the finest landscape in France, but none of it had evoked more than a sort of stunned, grudging admiration. For her the pattern had been set by the flat, tranquil plots of the *huerta*, with its gentle rustlings and splashings, with its generous harvests and the welcome shade inside the *barraca*. That was her model of landscape, not the truculent attractions of mountain crests and gorges, of waterfalls and sea cliffs.

Carmen and Manolo made it clear that they would be most reluctant to part with her. She pointed out that, now that Carmen was about to give up her work, they wouldn't need their 'grandmother' any more. 'An extra woman in the house just gets in the way,' she declared.

'So you want to go and get in your sister's way?'

'She wants me there.'

'We want you here.'

'She needs me there, more than you need me here now.'

'So you must go where you are most needed. It hasn't occurred to you, has it, just to do what pleases you, for a change?'

Teresa considered the matter. 'I think what pleases me is to be where I am most needed.'

Carmen sighed. 'Then I suppose it has to be the village again, beside your sister.'

Teresa wrote back, and booked her ticket for the following week. She dreaded the parting from her adopted family, and wanted to get it over as soon as possible. Once she was home she would have the *huerta* and her sister to console her. She would be able to see her own children and her grandchildren. How odd, that they would be strangers to her, less known and less loved than those she would be leaving behind.

The day before her departure, after some last minute shopping in the town centre, she was walking back so occupied with her inner landscape that she missed her usual turning, and found herself in an unfamiliar area of the city. She was in one of the poorer quarters, with groups of shabbily dressed people standing around or hurrying home from work. As she pushed her way through a group of loiterers a few words uttered in a familiar voice came to her. The speaker seemed to be seated at one of the café tables nearby, but at first she wasn't able to see him for the crowd. Not that she needed to. The ringing, angry tones were unmistakable, as was the subject matter – exploitation.

Gabriel was seated at a table with a few other men and, as usual, he was doing the talking. She was shocked by his appearance. My God, she thought, how old he looks! Old and sick and down at heel. Mechanically she walked on, unnoticed. When she came to the next corner she stopped, wondering what to do. She stood there for some moments, jostled by the crowd. Then she heaved a sad, perplexed sigh, and walked on. She said nothing about her dilemma when she got home.

The night that followed was one of the most sleepless she had ever known. Why, oh why, had she taken that wrong turning? If she'd gone home the usual way she'd never have seen him. She felt as if some force outside her had made her pass in front of him. The more she thought about it the more convinced she became that she was meant to see him. And if I was meant to see him, she reasoned, it must be because I was meant to do something about it. She wished she could just dismiss the matter from her mind. If only he hadn't looked so old. If only he hadn't looked so ill and down at heel. How could she go back to live in peace and comfort in her beloved *huerta*, leaving this ghost, this shadow of a man behind?

She got up very early and carefully unpacked the trunk she had filled the previous day. When Carmen appeared she told her she couldn't go just yet, and explained why.

'So you'll stay with us?'

'For the moment. Till I can speak to him. Till I see if he needs me.'

Carmen gave a little laugh. 'Perhaps I ought to break a leg,' she suggested.

'What on earth would you do that for?'

'Then I'd be the one that needed you most, and you'd stay here.'

'For a while,' Teresa conceded, smiling. 'But broken legs mend. I've a feeling that what's wrong with Gabriel won't mend that easily.'

That afternoon she went back to the café, determined to speak to Gabriel. But he wasn't there. She cursed herself for not having spoken the previous day. If she had, and he had neither wanted her nor needed her, she would be on her way back to Valencia by now.

She wrote a long letter to her sister, painfully setting out her reasons for the delay. Her husband looked ill, and tired and needy. She must find him and look after him if that was what was needed. Her sister's reply consisted of one sentence only – 'Would he do the same for you?' No, probably not. But that, after all, wasn't the problem.

Eventually she took her courage in both hands and went into the café. None of the waiters seemed to know anything about Gabriel. Soon they were all in a huddle, discussing the matter, while customers waited for attention. No one knew anything, but that didn't prevent them from going over all the possibilities again and again. Teresa left more depressed than ever.

Then one day, as she was walking past the café, one of the waiters called her.

'*Hé, madame, pstt, pstt.*' She edged her way among the crowded tables to where he stood, elegantly pouring out a *café au lait*. 'Your friend, there's a man here who knows him – *ce type-là* . . . ' and he pointed to a very seedy-looking middle-aged man who sat reading a paper in one of the darkest corners of the café.

The man stood up when Teresa approached and told him she was looking for Gabriel Mestres.

He bowed. 'I have the honour to be his friend.'

'Then please tell me where I can find him.'

The man's face acquired a suspicious expression.

'What for, may I inquire? Do you wish him well? Are you a friend?'

'I'm his wife,' she stated baldly, unprepared for this interrogation.

The man drew himself up to his full height, shook his head and waved a finger of denial right in front of Teresa's nose. 'Then I shall certainly not tell you where to find him.' And he folded his arms defiantly.

'But why not?'

'Because you are his wife. Because you have behaved abominably to him. *Voilà.*'

'But what did he say I did?'

'That, *madame*, you know better than anyone else.' In spite of his hostility the little man was evidently determined to hang on to the forms of courtesy.

'But I don't know, I really don't. Please tell me what I'm supposed to have done.' By this time the stress was telling on Teresa, and she felt so weak that she sat down on the nearest chair.

'Well, *madame*, if you force me to put it into words . . .

'At the end of the Spanish Civil War, ten years ago, your husband went into exile. You chose that moment to run away with a sergeant of the Civil Guard, a representative of the very oppressors he was fleeing from.'

Teresa was so outraged that she forgot about her faintness and stood up indignantly. She might have known Gabriel would invent some lurid tale to account for her absence.

Instead of denying the charge she merely asked, 'Do I look like the sort of woman a man would have run off with, even ten years ago?'

The little Frenchman was now on the horns of a dilemma. It would be manifestly absurd to claim that Teresa did look like that sort of woman. On the other hand, to admit the absurdity of this seemed lacking in gallantry. He spread out his hands in a deprecatory gesture. '*Ah, madame*,' he sighed, and shrugged gracefully.

'Besides,' continued Teresa, 'if you know my husband, you have no doubt found out that he is sometimes given to . . . to exaggeration, shall we say?'

'Yes indeed, *madame*. How well you put it.'

He was now won over, and invited her to sit down. It appeared that he and Gabriel had met through a common friend, and had sometimes shared a table at a café, but he hadn't been with them for some days because he was ill. Yes, he knew the address, and yes he would tell her. Perhaps the good God had sent his wife to him to comfort him in his last days. Well, to try and comfort him, if he would let her. '*Il n'est pas commode, votre mari.*'

Tired as she was, Teresa decided to go and see Gabriel right away. More than anything else she wanted to be done with the doubt and indecision.

She had to climb four flights of dark, ill-smelling stairs to reach his lodging house. The higher she went, the shabbier and dirtier her surroundings became.

She rang the bell and waited a moment. Then came a sound of shuffling and muttering, and ultimately the door was opened by the landlady in person, very much *en pantoufles*.

'Well?'

'Gabriel Mestres, please. Is he in?'

'Oh, you mean old Gabriel. Yes he's in, of course he's in. Where else would a sick man be but in his bed?'

'Is he very ill, then?'

'Yes, he's very ill. Of course he's ill. He's dying. Why do they all come here to die? One last week, another a couple of months ago . . . It's not very pleasant, I can tell you. Besides, it gives the place a bad name. Why must they all come here to die, tell me that?'

'Can I see him?'

'Please yourself. Along there.' The landlady jerked her head in the direction of a long, dark corridor. 'End room,' she flung over her shoulder as she shuffled back to the kitchen.

Teresa knocked on the door, trembling with apprehension.

'Come in, damn you,' was the reply. 'What is it now?'

Teresa opened the door and found Gabriel sitting propped up on the bed.

The room was small and filthy. It smelled of cheap tobacco, sweat and urine. The bedclothes were stained. The pillows against which the old man rested were even worse. And the occupant of the bed was a good match for his surroundings.

Since Teresa's earlier glimpse of him his appearance had deteriorated still further. He had a stubbly grey beard, and his hair was uncut and unkempt. Apart from a bright red spot on the middle of each cheek his face was deathly pale. But the eyes under their heavy brows still burned with their old fire. The source of his anger was evidently unquenched. He was scribbling something on a dirty sheet of paper, and didn't look up for a few seconds. When he did, his face registered little surprise.

'Well, what brings you here? Want to be in at the kill, I suppose. Who told you I was dying?'

'Nobody told me.'

'Liar! The landlady told you. I heard her, talking about people dying in her house. Well, I've a right to die where I please.'

'I didn't know. I heard you were here, and just came to see you.'

'Who told you?'

'Never mind.' She was surprised at her own daring in saying this. Ten years ago she couldn't have answered like that. 'I've just come to see you,' she repeated.

'Why, I wonder? After all these years. After the way you left me.'

'And after the way you left me. Don't forget that. At least I didn't tell lies about it afterwards.'

'Lies? What do you mean, lies? I told no lies about you. You weren't worth the effort.'

'What about the sergeant in the *Guardia Civil*? Where did he come in, then?'

For a moment Gabriel looked taken aback. Then he rallied. 'So that's who told you where I was! That little sneak of a Duchamps. Where did you meet up with him?'

'Never mind.' Having got away with this reply once before Teresa thought she would try it again. This time, however, it threw him into a paroxysm of fury.

'Get out!' he yelled. 'I don't want you here. I don't want to see you ever again. I don't know what you've come for, but you're not getting it, whatever it is. I don't care a damn about you or what you think or what you want. You can go to the devil.'

He seized a glass from the table near his bed and flung it at her. She managed to doge it, opened the door and hurried out, almost colliding with the landlady, who explained that she just happened to be passing.

Teresa asked her who was looking after Gabriel.

'*Parbleu*, he looks after himself. This isn't a first-class hotel, you know. Not a hospital either. More like a mortuary.'

Teresa pursued her line of inquiry.

'But his food, for instance, who sees to that?'

'His food? How should I know? He pays for his room, and only his room. He can either go out for his food or he can send my Berthe to the café for whatever he wants. There's no problem about his food. I have enough to do looking after my own family. It's not easy, running a place like this. Nothing but trouble, morning, noon and night. And then it seems I'm supposed to look after the sick and the dying as well! I tell you . . . '

'*Hé, la patronne!* Shut your bloody trap. I'm sick to death, yes, to death, of your whining.' The voice from the other side of the door was startlingly powerful for so sick a man.

The landlady shook her head. 'He will die shouting, that one.'

'Perhaps he isn't dying after all,' suggested Teresa. The landlady gave her a disgusted look. It seemed that neither prospect was to her liking.

Teresa hurried away, feeling she had been defeated on all fronts. She had failed to establish any kind of rapport with her husband, and she had also proved unable to get any kind of help for him from the landlady.

By the time she got home she had settled in her mind that she must make another attempt. Perhaps Gabriel would get over his initial hostility, especially if he saw how much he stood to gain. But then she shook her head doubtfully. Gain had never been much of an object to Gabriel, she had to admit. He had always been inclined to do himself as much damage as possible, for the sheer joy of disagreement. He would enter into conflict with anyone, all the more vigorously if he was likely to be the loser.

Still, she must try.

That evening she consulted Carmen and Manolo. After some discussion her friends suggested that she should bring Gabriel back to the house, where she could look after him properly. She was deeply grateful for the suggestion, though not at all sure that it would work.

The next morning she set out again for the lodging house, carrying a bowl of chickpea stew.

The door was opened by a ten-year-old waif, presumably Berthe. The child stared at her in silence and watched as she went along to Gabriel's room. This time she knocked and went in without waiting for an answer. Gabriel was again sitting up in bed, and his eyes were on her as soon as she opened the door.

'So it's you again. Didn't I tell you to go to the devil?'

'Well, I have,' snapped Teresa. A momentary gleam in his eye gave her the idea that he was enjoying the joke. Perhaps if she'd been able to stand up to him before, to meet him on his own ground . . . But just now she had a mission to carry out. This was no time for dangerous experiments.

'I've brought you some *cocido*,' she said, 'the way you used to like it. It's still quite hot.'

She placed the bowl on the table near the bed and was looking round for a fork when a chuckle from Gabriel made her turn round. She was just in time to see him turning the bowl upside down, spilling all the contents on to the already filthy floor.

'Is that all you came for?' he asked coolly.

Teresa felt tempted to give up. But looking at him in silence she noticed the air of utter weariness with which he lay back against the pillows after his small effort. A wave of pity flooded over her, and she decided she must try again.

'Gabriel,' she said gently, 'I can see you're ill, and this is a horrible room, and there's no one to look after you. I tried to persuade the landlady to do something for you, but it's no use.'

Gabriel muttered, 'That old cow!' Then he sat silent, staring straight ahead of him at the closed door. Encouraged by his silence she went on. 'We've decided, the family I live with and I, that the best thing would be for you to come and live with us. I could look after you. You'd get whatever treatment you require, rest, good food . . . ' Her voice trailed away, and she waited nervously for his answer. When it came it was not in the usual bellow of rage.

He spoke quietly, almost as if slightly amused:

'So that's what you've come for? To humiliate me with your charity? You and your well-off friends.'

'They're not well off. They're ordinary working folk.'

'They're well off if they can afford to feed an extra mouth. Woman, where have you been living all this time? Have you forgotten what it's like to be poor?' His voice was slowly getting louder. 'Have you forgotten how the rich exploit us, day in day out, and then rub salt in the wound by offering us charity? Tell your filthy friends I'd rather starve to death in a garret than accept one crumb of bread from them.' By now he was well on the way to his habitual bellow, but was stopped by a fit of coughing.

Teresa broke the silence which followed.

'You haven't changed, Gabriel.'

'Well, you have,' he gasped, 'you've grown old and ugly.'

Teresa was inexpressibly hurt. She tried to keep her voice as even as she could. 'I meant you haven't learnt anything. Still cutting off your nose to spite your face.'

'And you,' he said, 'you're a woman of no principles. An opportunist. You've sold yourself to the enemy. You'll live in comfort and I'll die in poverty. But I know which of us I'd rather be.'

Teresa couldn't help feeling that there was a touch of grandeur in the old man's attitude.

'And now you can leave me,' he added quietly.

'Yes, I'll leave you,' she said. 'And this time I know exactly why I'm doing it.'

As she closed the bedroom door behind her she heard a loud thud followed by a crash. 'The bowl,' she thought. 'I forgot to pick it up.'

The girl was still hanging around in the hall and seemed unmoved by the noise. Flying crockery was evidently a normal part of her daily life.

As she hurried down the stairs Teresa felt an odd mixture of disappointment, relief and humiliation. She was sorry she had not been able to persuade him, relieved that the whole episode was over, and humiliated because she had not been straight with him. By telling him that this time she knew why she was leaving him she had implied that it was because of his outrageous behaviour. But deep down she knew it was because of the hurt she had felt when he had called her old and ugly.

But what did it matter, anyway?

There was no way of bridging the gap between them. Now they would never meet again. She would have the life she wanted, back in the *huerta* with her sister, and he would have the death he wanted, alone in his mean little room, with his pride and his fury to see him through to the end.

2

The Path

Why is it always so much more difficult to come down? You get to the top thinking all your troubles are over, and then it's even worse on the way down. This time, Jim realized, it was because of the narrowness of the path, combined with its hard, slippery surface. And the odd loose stone didn't help matters, either.

Still, there was nothing to worry about. Just a case of being careful.

The path was no more than eighteen inches wide at some stretches. On his right he had the side of the mountain, rising abruptly – a wall of grass and stony outcrops. On his left, a sheer drop down to the road a few hundred feet below.

He hadn't meant to stop on his journey, still less start climbing. But he had been beguiled by the sight of this path clinging to the side of the mountain. So he parked in front of the little inn and got out, just to have a look. Wondering how far the path went, he started climbing. He could see it in front of him, beckoning him on, till eventually it disappeared round the side of the hill. He would go on till he got to that bend, just to see what happened then. It would probably peter out at that point. It didn't look at all like a man-made path. Just a geological accident, so there was no reason to expect it to go all the way to the top.

It didn't. Eventually it did come to an end, as he had imagined, but not before he had been climbing for nearly half an hour. Quite suddenly the path, which had maintained its width fairly evenly so far, narrowed to a few inches, and then disappeared. There was nothing for it but to turn back.

By this time the mists had come swirling in below him, so it was hard to tell how high he had climbed. But from the magnificent view of peak after peak that had opened out to him above the bed of mist, he knew he had climbed a fair height.

He wasn't worried about the mist. The only place the path could take him was back down to the inn and his car. No possibility of taking the wrong turning. He was absolutely sure that no path had branched off at any point. So there was nothing to worry about.

The only tricky thing was the actual getting down the path. He wasn't really equipped for this sort of terrain. His town shoes slipped and skidded rather easily on the bare rock, and the soles were too thin. He could feel each irregularity of the surface, and suspected that a few blisters were on the way. Worst of all was the presence of loose stones on the path. On his way up this had been a mild annoyance. Coming down it constituted a definite danger. Putting the brakes on is a lot easier when you're going up, with gravity on your side, as it were.

It was all right, really, in the stretches where the path widened out a little. But he knew he must soon come to the bit where it maintained a width of no more than eighteen inches for a long way, between one bend and the next. At that point he knew that every step would be a hazard.

He rounded a bend and saw the long, narrow stretch ahead of him. For at least fifty yards it was going to be pretty tricky going. Well, he would just have to take it easy, very easy. Luckily he wasn't in a hurry.

Just keep your eyes on the path and watch what you're doing, he told himself. And don't get carried away by the scenery. You can have a good look when the path widens again round the next corner. Just concentrate on the job in hand.

He was concentrating, putting his whole being into the business of picking his way down, step by step, when something made him look a little further along.

In front of him, about ten yards ahead, the path was completely blocked by a burly figure. Suddenly Jim found himself gazing at what appeared to be the prototype of the wild Highlandman of old.

The man was tall, and remarkably broad. He had little hair on his head, but a great deal of it attached to his face, in the shape of an unkempt reddish beard. His right hand clutched a heavy staff. A tattered kilt revealed two massive knees above a pair of muscular calves. The general impression was of strength, weight, and an unyielding disposition. He was standing in what looked like an attitude of defiance, scowling at this effete insect that had got across his path. He looked as if he was ready to advance at any moment and sweep the encumbrance out of the way with one thrust of his staff.

Jim reflected nervously that the only direction in which he could be thrust by the menacing stick was a sharply downward one.

The two men stared at each other for some time, without exchanging a word of greeting. It never even occurred to Jim to treat this as a normal encounter. From the first second of seeing the man he had been convinced of the stranger's hostility. The Highlandman was gazing at him with attention, weighing him up. Then he drew himself up to his full height and began advancing up the path again, as if Jim wasn't there.

Automatically Jim flattened himself against the side of the hill. It might just be possible for the two men to squeeze past each other, and he certainly wasn't going to be the one on the outside. Not if he could help it.

The man stopped when he was about a foot away from Jim. With a gesture of the head he indicated that Jim was to move to the outside of the path. Jim flattened himself even further against the hillside and shook his head.

The man growled. It was just that, a growl, not in any sense an attempt at a recognizable word. To his surprise Jim found himself growling back. He would never have believed himself capable of making such a sound.

With another growl, the man raised his stick and thrust it between Jim's back and the wall of rock he was leaning against. Then he moved it to the side, in a gently prising motion that separated Jim a few inches from the wall.

And then the man smiled. Jim would have liked to believe that this smile betokened a friendly intent on the stranger's part, but he found it rather easier to interpret it as an expression of gloating anticipation. Then the stranger placed himself next to Jim, also with his back to the wall, and, using his staff as a lever, prised Jim a little further forward. It was clear that he expected Jim to edge past him.

Jim found himself speaking in a strange, cracked voice. 'I wouldn't bother going any further. It's too misty now. No view.'

'It's not the view I'm after.'

'Oh!'

The man was looking at him severely, tapping his foot impatiently. Jim decided that the best thing to do was go back up the path to where it was wide enough for two people to pass in safety. He felt sure there was no point in suggesting they conduct the operation in the other direction. This man was not going to turn back.

Without speaking, he turned to start going up the path again. But just as he was taking his first step he was brought to a halt by the man's hand, clutching him fiercely by the upper arm. The grip was so ferocious that he cried out in pain.

'I was only going back up a little, where there's room to pass.'

'There's room to pass here. And this is where we met.' The man had let go of his arm. Again he made the gesture with his head, inviting Jim to move past him.

Jim looked at the width of the path and looked at the width of the man as he stood leaning up against the side of the hill, and shook his head. He could just manage to find room for his feet; but the man's girth accounted for all the available room higher up. There was no way Jim could get past him without leaning out over the precipice.

'Can't be done,' he announced tersely.

'It can,' was the equally terse reply.

Without saying another word the man placed the end of his staff between his feet, holding the top with both hands.

'Go ahead,' he said.

Yes, thought Jim, it could be done. If he held on to the staff he could edge past the man, leaning over the precipice. His antagonist looked immovably firm. He knew his own weight would count as nothing against this rock of a man. Yes, it could be done. Provided the rock in question held firm, of course. He had no doubts about the man's body weight. What he simply couldn't fathom was the strange creature's intentions.

He was wondering whether he could afford to trust him, when the man said, 'Now,' and Jim put his hand tentatively on the staff. He would just have to trust him.

Before moving out over the abyss he pulled hard on the staff with both hands. It held firm.

It can't have taken him many seconds to complete the manoeuvre. It felt like years. Years of moving his feet along,

44

an inch at a time, with his face only a few inches away from his tormentor's. He could feel the man's breath on his face, and the wave of warmth that emanated from him. The man's eyes were fixed on the distance ahead. Even when Jim's face passed right in front, the eyes never blinked, never gave any sign. And the staff remained utterly firm.

As soon as the operation was over the man continued his ascent. There were a thousand questions Jim wanted to ask him – who are you, where are you going, why have you done this to me? But he was too weak to do anything but continue the journey down, slowly, painfully, trembling with fear and apprehension. The descent was still dangerous, and how did he know the man wouldn't turn and come back and force him to go through the whole nightmare again?

On his way up he had toyed with the idea of going in to the inn when he got back down again, for a rest and a hot drink. But his horror of the whole place was so great that as soon as he got back to the road he more or less fell into the car and drove off. It was foolish, he knew. After all, he was perfectly safe now, and it would have been a good idea to ask about the man. Surely the locals must know him. He would have given a lot to know who he was, and why he had behaved in this way. But not today. No, not today. He wouldn't feel happy till he had put many miles between himself and this uncanny place.

Perhaps on his way back south he would stop and ask.

That night, in his hotel room, surrounded by city streets and the welcome clamour of city traffic, he began to wonder whether he had imagined the whole thing. Or had he fallen asleep in the car when he stopped for a rest and dreamed it all? The whole episode seemed too surreal to be possible. Was it some creation of his subconscious, trying to teach him something? And what did the mountain stand for? And the man, my God, what did the man stand for?

In the end he came to the conclusion that the message was that you have to face your fears. His subconscious, either in a dream or in some strange sort of a vision, had forced him to do what he most dreaded. None of his attempts at escape had been of any avail. And the lesson to be learned was that if you trust yourself to the terror you can come through unscathed. For after all it was the wild Highlandman who had made it possible for him to get past, by keeping his staff firm for him to hold on to. Yes, his wild man of the mountains, his Shadow, in Jungian terms, had been no more than an image of his own fears. That must be it.

Having arrived at this explanation, and feeling relatively satisfied that this was the solution, he decided to go to bed. He began to undress, and was surprised to feel a pain in his left arm as he pulled off his sweater. He took off his shirt and had a look. On the upper arm was a series of sharply defined little bruises, four in front and one behind.

3

Boister

'You wouldn't be minding about the dog, would you, sir?'

'The dog?'

'At night, I mean. He always sleeps in this room.'

George felt that perhaps he might be minding about the dog. He wasn't very keen on dogs in general, and he'd never even met this one.

'Oh, well. I'll just make sure the door's properly shut.'

The woman shook her head. 'He'll only scratch,' she said.

George decided to try a different approach. 'Well, what about the other guests? How do they usually tackle the problem?'

'To tell you the truth, sir, there's never been any other guests. I've only just started doing Bed and Breakfast, and you're the first. Would you be wanting an evening meal, sir?'

George wasn't too sure about an evening meal from a landlady who was a self-proclaimed novice. But it was already getting dark. He reflected that it was too late to start looking for something else, and told her he would be wanting an evening meal.

Mrs Bell left him to get on with his unpacking, which he did with some hesitation. Things didn't look too auspicious so far. Here he was, unpacking his things in a dreary room, with no doubt an equally dreary meal ahead of him, and with a dog as a prospective room mate. But then, he hadn't come with any great expectations. His doctor had insisted that he must take a short holiday, so here he was, ready to explore the Scottish Highlands.

As soon as he had got his things in order he went down to the sitting room, which was a shade less austere than his bedroom. A minute later Mrs Bell came in to see that the fire was burning all right. With her appeared the dog, a large, dishevelled creature of indeterminate breed. It trotted up to George in an uninhibited manner which he found a little alarming. He wasn't exactly afraid of dogs, but they did fill him with certain misgivings, especially where the large, expansive kind was concerned.

'What's he called?' George felt they should at least be introduced, since they were to share a room.

'Boister, sir. He came to us as a stray, and my husband christened him Boister, as we didn't know his real name.'

'I see.'

Doubt as to the logic of this reasoning must have tinged George's voice, for the woman added almost apologetically, 'It's not a proper name, I know.'

'Very appropriate,' commented George, leaving Mrs Bell to decide where the appropriateness lay.

After the landlady had left the room Boister settled in front of the fire, and he and George paid no further attention to each other.

George's thoughts were back again in the narrow channel in which they had been stuck for the last three months.

Melanie, Melanie, he just couldn't get the damned girl out of his mind. Or rather, out of his heart.

Up till now the expressions 'heartbroken' and 'heavy-hearted' had seemed to him to be merely a poetic way of expressing sadness. Now he knew just how right, how physiologically right, they were. For months he had had this almost physical weight on his heart, the nagging pain in his chest, just where he assumed his heart was located, as if the very muscle itself had been bruised and battered. The sensation was there all day, kept him awake most of the night, weighed on him during his few hours of troubled sleep, and in the morning it was with him from the first moment of consciousness. In fact, the pain was the consciousness, as if nothing else existed for him. He longed for a moment of respite. If he could even forget the pain for one moment, he felt it would be less unbearable when it came back.

And along with the pain was the anger, the humiliation of being told by the girl he'd been sleeping with for the past year, that she'd got tired of him and didn't want to see him any more.

He tried to work on this, to drive the pain out by concentrating on the anger, and cherished a number of fantasies that all ended in his putting Melanie down savagely. He wanted to destroy her self-esteem as she had destroyed his.

He tried drowning his sorrow in work, but even that never seemed to drive the pain away. Still, if it brought him promotion, if it helped to put him in a position in which Melanie might regret having rejected him, it would be worth all the effort.

And he worked and worked, till he collapsed. So here he was with his misery, in a cold, strange house, in the middle of a brooding glen, with nothing on earth to look forward to for the next ten days, not even work.

As his reflections reached this stage he gave an enormous sigh. Boister leapt up, rushed over to him, gave the side of his face a long, loving lick, and settled down in front of him, with his head on George's knees, looking up at him with his melting brown eyes.

'Oh, Boister!' whispered George, 'I'm so miserable!'

And he burst into tears. He sat and cried for a long time, while Boister gazed at him with big, mournful eyes, occasionally snuffling gently, as if in sympathy.

The thought that Mrs Bell might appear at any moment with the meal eventually helped him to pull himself together. He sat patting Boister gently on the head, having lost all his distrust of the dog, and feeling lightened by his tears.

When the meal was ready he sat at the table, convinced that he wasn't at all hungry. But the food was astonishingly good, and daintily served, and he enjoyed it. At the end he complimented his hostess on her cuisine.

'I was cook up at the big house for years,' she explained. Suddenly he understood the reason for her deferential manner of speaking. She had been a servant, and he clearly belonged to the class of the served rather than the serving. 'And my husband was gardener there too, till he retired a few years ago,' she went on. 'And then, soon after retiring, he got cancer, and died a couple of months ago. That's why I decided to do B-and-B.'

As she was about to leave the room she said, 'I'll come back about nine o'clock with a cup of tea.'

'Oh, that won't be necessary, thank you.'

Mrs Bell looked quite shocked.

'Oh, but I must give you your cup of tea. All the landladies do. I wouldn't like to be less than the others.'

George accepted the prospect of a cup of tea at nine o'clock so that Mrs Bell need not be shamed in her profession, and after that ceremony was over he decided on an early night. As soon as he stood up Boister leapt up and preceded him to the bedroom. George reflected with some surprise that he was really quite looking forward to having the dog's company.

It was cold in the bedroom, and he undressed quickly and got into bed, followed at once by Boister, who snuggled up beside him near the foot of the bed, with his head resting on George's ankles. The arrangement at least had the advantage of warmth.

He woke up some time later feeling rather less warm. Boister had wriggled into the middle of the bed, and George found himself perched along the edge.

He got up and surveyed the situation. Boister was sleeping peacefully in the middle of the bed, and George realized that if he followed the adage and let this particular sleeping dog lie, all that was going to be left for him was the choice as to which edge of the bed he was to lie on. He decided to try and move the dog without waking him. By gently tugging at the bedclothes he managed to bring him close enough to one side of the bed to leave a reasonable amount of room at the other.

He walked round the bed to the vacant side, and was just about to get in, when Boister gave a huge sigh, stretched voluptuously, and rolled back into the middle. George accepted defeat. He put on a warm sweater and crawled into what little space was left for him. After all, it was only for one night.

In the morning he woke up surprisingly refreshed. It hadn't been such a bad night after all. Boister greeted him with a good-morning lick, and George reciprocated with a few hearty slaps on the animal's back. He felt that they had established a pretty good working relationship.

He told Mrs Bell that he would leave after breakfast, and she asked him whether he would like a packed lunch for his journey. Before answering he looked out of the window and saw the side of the glen rising steeply behind the house, with a ray of sun slanting through the trees. It seemed a pity not to go out and explore before leaving. Suppose he climbed to the top of the hill and got a bit of a view? After all, it didn't matter what time he left. Besides, he wanted just a little more time with Boister. For the first time for months he felt in some way bound to another living being, and he was reluctant to abandon the relationship.

He told Mrs Bell he might do a little exploring before driving off. 'And I'll take that packed lunch with me.' Then, casually, as if it had just occurred to him, he added, 'Would Boister like to come with me, do you think?'

Oh, yes. Boister would certainly enjoy that!

When he came back downstairs, booted and dressed for the heights, he found Boister lying in front of the kitchen fire. The dog wagged an indolent tail.

'Come on, Boister!'

The dog was up like a shot.

They set off at once, and soon started climbing, through woods at first, then over grass, then stumbling over clumps of heather, pushing their way through bracken as high as George's shoulders. Boister was invisible most of the time, but audible.

The more they climbed, the more the top of the hill seemed to recede, and the more obstacles he found in his way – streams, bogs, patches of dense woodland, sudden deep crevices, huge boulders. Again and again he thought he was about to reach the summit, but he always found another crest rising in front of him. He was tired, and felt sure he ought to turn back. But the lure of the summit, and his fear of yet another failure, even in so small a thing, kept him struggling on. And Boister was charging merrily ahead, looking back every so often, panting encouragement to him.

At last, when he'd stopped thinking about it and was just plodding on mechanically, he suddenly found himself on a small plateau, with the land falling away from him on every side.

Boister was running round and round the flat area of the

summit, obviously happy and excited. George looked for a suitable boulder and sat down, so surprised at this sudden end to the struggle that he could hardly believe he'd made it to the top. Looking round he saw range upon range of hills – or were these not mountains, actually? – and a sense of triumph and wonder flooded over him.

'Boister,' he said, 'we've done it. How about some lunch?'

It wasn't till he was half-way through his sandwiches that he realized that the pain had gone and the weight had lifted, not just partially, but completely. As soon as he thought about it, of course, the pain came back. But at least he had had the first break-through. Some day the pain would go for good.

It was late afternoon before he got back, and he was very glad he had made it before dark. Mrs Bell seemed relieved to see him, and expressed astonishment and some concern when he told here where he'd been.

'But that's a rough climb, sir! And in November, and all alone!'

'Well, I had Boister. And I think, as it's so late, perhaps I'll just spend another night here, if I may.'

'Yes, of course, sir. Boister will be pleased.'

George felt a little glow of pleasure at these words. It was comforting to be liked and appreciated, even if only by a dog. After a moment he decided that the last phrase was a piece of unjustifiable speciesism, and apologized mentally to Boister.

The following morning he set off again with the dog, in another direction this time. Again it was nearly dark before he got back, and he decided to stay on for another night. On the third day he told Mrs Bell he would like to stay on for the rest of his holiday.

He spent the time wandering about with Boister, grateful

for the companionship that asked for no explanations, that made no demands except for the very elementary ones, such as taking the best part of the bed to sleep in.

When his ten days were up he left the glen with regret. He felt healed by the presence of the mountains, by Boister's companionship, even by Mrs Bell's sparse, matter-of-fact conversation. It was all so different from what he was going back to. Once he left these things behind he was afraid the bitterness and pain might come back. But perhaps, after this cleansing, the pain might come with less bitterness.

He had not been back long when Melanie phoned. The conversation started off as an almost word-for-word repeat of one of his vicious little fantasies. Only, he didn't take the chance and put her down, when she came to the bit about being miserable and lonely. He didn't suggest a reconciliation, either, for he suddenly realized that this was no longer what he wanted. Instead he decided to do the magnanimous thing, and pass on his remedy for a broken heart.

'Look, Mel,' he said, 'I've just had ten days in the Highlands. There's a wonderful dog there . . . '

'Did you say doc?'

'No. Dog. The canine variety. He's called Boister . . . '

The click at the end of the line informed him that Melanie had hung up.

He sighed and gave a little shrug. Melanie, it seemed, wasn't ready for Boister.

4

The Urn

As soon as she heard her father beginning to snore, Elena raised herself on one elbow and listened more attentively, hoping to hear a change in her mother's quieter breathing. It was always hard to tell, with the noise of the snoring going on. Once again, she would just have to chance it.

Silently she got up and glided towards the open door.

'Elena, where are you going?' came the urgent whisper from her mother.

'I'm just going out for a breath of fresh air. I've got a bad headache.' Elena had her answer ready. It would at least serve to avoid a crisis.

'If you're not back inside two minutes I'll send your father after you. And you know what he'll have to say about it.'

Elena stood outside the door, fighting the temptation to make a run for the forest and the waiting Manolo. Gradually she mastered her impatience and went back in. After all, the longer she stayed outside, the longer it would be before her mother allowed herself to fall asleep.

Once inside again, she was tormented by the thought that she would have to wait a long time before she dare try again. To think that she should be held back tonight, just when she had her awe-inspiring secret to tell Manolo.

The room felt intolerably hot and stuffy. Her limbs ached, and every part of the bed that was in contact with her body seemed made of burning coals. Yet she hardly dared stir, afraid that any movement might increase her mother's vigilance.

During the past three months Elena had learned many little devices to allay parental suspicion. Now she was inspired to try out a new ruse. She began to breathe slowly and heavily, imitating the pattern of her mother's breathing in sleep, with a little pause after each exhalation. She had no guarantee that she herself sounded like that when she was asleep, but it was worth trying.

And it seemed to work, for soon she heard a similar rhythm coming from her mother's corner of the room, forming a syncopated pattern with her own breathing and her father's snores.

Cautiously she got up again, stole out of the house and ran on tiptoe to the entrance of the forest path that led to the next village two miles away. She was so late tonight that she expected Manolo to be very near by now, impatiently waiting for her. At every step she was sure she would find herself in his arms, with all her fears and anxiety gone, telling him her wonderful secret.

Since their last meeting four days ago, she had become convinced that she was pregnant. They had spoken about this possibility and had agreed that it would be the best thing that could possibly happen.

'You'll see,' Manolo had said, 'they'll make the most terrible fuss, both your parents and mine, but in the end they'll all agree that the only thing to do is to let us get married right away.'

They both knew it would be a case of putting up with a few days of hard words and recriminations, and then it would all simmer down and they would be married.

She walked on quickly, eager to find her lover, thinking that perhaps he had decided to wait for her in their love nest, a little clearing in the forest half-way between their two villages. As she moved along, guided by the patches of moonlight that fell on the path here and there, she thought yet again with wonder of this love that had transformed her life, turning her girlhood into womanhood in a matter of hours.

She had first seen Manolo at the yearly fair in the big town six months ago. He was with a group of young men, some of whom she knew. Elena learned from one of her friends that he was the son of a family that had recently moved into the neighbouring village of Las Espinas.

He had not spoken to any of the girls; but as they moved about the stalls they kept coming across him. And every time she saw him she noticed that his eyes were on her, grave, unsmiling and intense. Every time she remembered this look a flutter of excitement would tremble in her throat.

When he appeared at her home on the third day, she was not surprised.

Manolo had come to ask her father about one of the crops grown in the area, explaining that this particular crop had not been grown where he had come from. His parents had heard that Elena's father was an expert on the subject, and had sent him along to ask for advice.

While the two men talked, Elena and her mother were busy about their household tasks.

'Look, I'll show you what the seed is like when it's ready to sow.' Elena's father got up and crossed the room to take a handful of grain out of one of the sacks ranged on the floor.

Manolo seized the opportunity to turn and look at Elena. As their eyes met the girl felt the absolute conviction that her fate had been decided.

She knew he could not speak to her in her father's presence unless the father himself brought her into the conversation. And this, she realized, would certainly not happen.

In that moment the first impulse of deviousness was born in the girl. She waited till it was clear that the conversation was about to come to an end. Then she picked up the large earthenware urn, with the intention of filling it at the well. Manolo would have to pass that way to get to the path. Outside, away from the paternal presence, he would be able to speak to her.

As she picked up the heavy urn, she realized she had set herself a difficult task, for it was more than half-full of water. She would have to carry it very carefully, not to spill any, and yet at the same time she would have to appear to be carrying it effortlessly, as if it were empty.

She braced herself and lifted it up lightly with one hand.

'Where are you going?' Her father stuck a foot out in front of her, bringing her to a sudden halt which set up a gentle, splashing noise inside the urn. She answered quickly to cover the sound:

'I'm going for water.'

'But you've already got water this morning.'

'Yes, but I spilt some. We need more.'

The foot was withdrawn. Elena stepped across the threshold, poised, upright, apparently relaxed. As she walked to the well she could hear that her father had come to the door to say good-bye to the guest, so she didn't dare relax her control of the heavy urn.

By the time she got to the well her arm was aching badly. But it didn't matter. Manolo was coming, she could hear his steps approaching. When the footsteps ceased she turned and looked round, and their eyes met again.

She filled the metal cup that always stood by the well and offered it to Manolo.

'Will you drink?'

He took the cup, drank from it, and handed it back to her still half full.

'For you,' he said.

Solemnly she drank, then looked up at him again.

'I must speak to my father,' he said. 'Then I'll come back.'

She nodded and he turned and went on his way, taking the narrow path through the woods.

After he had gone she looked into the water and said to her reflection;

'I am betrothed.'

It seemed strange and wonderful and utterly inevitable, as if she had always known this was to happen.

The following day he came and asked for her hand. Her parents raised only one objection – she was too young. With this civil war on it would be too risky to let such a young girl leave her own home. All Manolo's assurances that she would be just as safe in his home were of no avail. Las Espinas, Elena's father pointed out, was nearer enemy territory. There had already been a raid there the previous year. It was not safe.

In the end it was agreed that they were to wait for two years before they were married.

Meanwhile Manolo was allowed to come and see her every Sunday evening. They sat side by side at the front door. They spoke little, and never touched, apart from the regulation handshake at greeting and parting.

But the strain of being so close and yet so divided, of having so much to say to each other that could not be said in the company of others, became almost intolerable. Elena sensed that Manolo felt it as keenly as she did.

One evening as he was taking leave he managed to whisper a single word to her. 'Midnight,' he breathed, and gave a quick look in the direction of the path. Elena understood.

Now, after three months of intermittent clandestine meetings, Elena was hurrying along, eager to discuss the probability of an early release. As Manolo said, they would have a stormy time to go through. But the happy ending was certain. After all, it was only Elena's parents who insisted on delay, and how could they possibly want anything other than a speedy wedding, if their daughter was pregnant?

She came to the little clearing and Manolo was not there. She knew she was much later than usual, but surely Manolo would not have given up and gone home? After waiting for a quarter of an hour in growing impatience and anxiety, she decided to go on to his village. This part of the path was less familiar to her, so she advanced cautiously, feeling just a little nervous. When she reached the last bend in the path, just before the clearing in the forest where Las Espinas began, she stopped, afraid of being seen in the moonlight by some wakeful neighbour.

It was strange how silent everything was in the village. In the forest she could hear the usual small nocturnal noises, but over the village absolute silence reigned. Not a voice, not even the barking of a dog. Nothing. Thick black silence.

Elena shuddered. Her impatience had gradually given way to frustration. Now suddenly this frustration turned to panic.

Sobbing with terror she began to run back the way she had come, stumbling and tripping over roots and stones, feeling the waiting branches catching at her clothes, tangling in her hair.

Just before reaching the love nest she fell and lay panting for a while. Suddenly she was overcome by the fear that she might harm the child in her flight. Slowly she got up and hobbled to the love nest, determined to wait there as long as she dare stay out.

She simply couldn't imagine why Manolo had not come. Something terrible must have happened to prevent him. What if his parents had found out about their meetings? Had his father perhaps locked him up? But this seemed unlikely. And if he had met with an accident someone would surely have come to tell her – after all, they were officially betrothed.

The night wore on, and still she waited. Shortly before dawn she realized she would have to go home, or face certain discovery. She left their love nest with a sad premonition. They would never meet there again, she felt sure.

Very early in the morning, just as she was sinking into a troubled sleep, she became aware of a great commotion in the village. She struggled up and stumbled to the door, just as her parents were hurrying out.

Word had come that Las Espinas had been attacked by the rebels the previous evening, just after nightfall. All the men had been killed, and the women and children taken prisoner.

'That silence,' she murmured, 'that terrible silence!'

Her mother caught her as she fell to the ground unconscious. When she came round she was told that her father had gone off with the other men to bury the dead. Later that day, when they came back, they confirmed the tragic story. All the men had indeed been killed. Manolo had been found lying beside the bodies of his father and his brothers, just outside their house.

Elena spent the next two days in bed, feverish and weeping. She kept thinking of all she had been doing that evening and that night, while Manolo already lay dead outside his own front door. She thought of how she had longed for this meeting even more furiously than ever before, with her newly confirmed secret to share with him. She thought of her long hours of waiting in growing fear and dread, and of her wild flight through the forest. And above all she thought of the silence, the terrible silence of death that had hung over the village.

On the third day her mother told her it was time to get up and stop crying.

'I can't!' she sobbed. And at that moment her crying stopped. She had been trying for some time to control it, to no avail. Her mother's quiet, firm words had had the required effect. Suddenly the storm was over.

Elena stood in front of the little mirror at the sink, combing her long hair. She would have to tell her parents about the child. The new life she had been looking forward to was starting now. She would have to put up with the scoldings and recriminations alone, without the wedding to look forward to and without Manolo. But she would have the child. That would be her new life.

She put her hand on her breast and felt her heart beating, and thought of the new heartbeat inside her. She would be very careful, she would treat her body with respect, with reverence.

As she crossed over to the door she remembered how she had walked across the very same tiles carrying the heavy urn that first day Manolo had come.

Once again she stepped over the threshold, poised, upright, relaxed.

5

Epitaph

The place seemd to proclaim the ultimate triumph of death. A graveyard, yes, and a dying graveyard at that, in the middle of a dying Scottish glen.

Long ago there must have been some sort of community here. The ruined church would be the centre from which roads and paths radiated out to the farms and hamlets for miles around. Now there was nothing, just the odd ruin here and there to show where a thriving farm or a humble cottage had been.

The church looked as if it had survived for longer. But even here the roof had fallen in, the walls were crumbling, the pews had been carried off, some for firewood perhaps, others to make a handsome mantelpiece in some new home. The pulpit had gone – dismembered, no doubt. After all, what would you do with a pulpit anywhere else?

For a while the woman stood still, looking into the church, and trying to think of what you could do with a displaced pulpit.

She turned away from the church, telling herself as she stood looking out at the drowsy graveyard that this was no place for these frivolous thoughts. She was in the presence of death – not just the death of the church and the graveyard, but the death of the whole glen.

Years ago this place had teemed with life. Men working in the fields, women busy at home, children gathered together in the school – for there must have been a school – laughing and shouting in the playground, the clip-clop of horses' hooves on the road, the hedges well tended, flourishing, the young corn growing strong and green, taller every day.

She saw herself approaching one of the cottages. A dog barked, a small child hurried into the house, afraid of this stranger, some chickens made off in a frightened flurry. She stood in the doorway and called out, and sniffed the glorious smell of new-baked bread.

Then a young woman came to the door, with a baby at her breast.

She looked at the visitor in some surprise. 'Yes?'

'I've come to talk to you, if I may.'

'Where from?'

'From the twentieth century.'

The young woman shook her head, not understanding.

'How did you get here?'

'By car. I've left it beside the church.'

'Left what?'

'My car. But you don't know about cars, do you?'

The young woman shook her head again.

'I don't know, I just don't know. Who are you?'

'I'm Margaret Evesham.'

'So you must be a woman, if you're called Margaret. But why are you dressed like a man?'

'The trousers, you mean? We all do, nowadays.'

'Why? Don't you like being a woman?'

'Oh, yes. Well, not always. But that's not why we wear trousers. At least, I don't think it is.'

Now sure of her visitor's sex, the young woman unbent a little.

'I'm Jenny Hyslop,' she said. 'Would you like to come in?'

The conversation was at first disappointing. There were

too many gaps, too many explanations to give. But gradually the two women found common ground in the subject of children, husbands, family.

By the time Margaret left she felt as if she were leaving a sister behind. It was odd how at home she had felt after the first few minutes. Everything seemed familiar, and loved and reassuring. Here, she knew, were her roots. This woman's experience was in some obscure way exactly her own. She left feeling that she had known Jenny Hyslop all her life – even from before her life. Jenny and her mother, and her grandmother, and whole generations of simple country women were as much a part of her as her own complicated and restless experience. And this knowledge filled her with a great sense of peace and confidence. The words 'Life goes on' had suddenly taken on a new, wider meaning.

Yes, she thought, *life goes on*. Not only the life of the living, but also the life of the dead.. And when our turn comes . . .

Once again she found herself standing on the threshold of the ruined church, looking out at the silent glen. She felt comforted, and realized only now how deep her need of comfort had been.

Slowly she moved forward among the fallen gravestones. Most were covered with lichen, illegible. She stopped in front of one of the smaller, humbler stones. On an impulse she picked up a piece of broken slate that must have fallen many years ago from the church roof, and carefully scraped off the lichen.

Only a few words remained legible.

' . . . *and of his wife, Jenny Hyslop, aged* . . . '

At the very foot of the stone were a few more legible words, apparently from a biblical text:

' . . . *ould not perish, but have eve as ng l fe.*'

6

Prize Plots

It isn't always easy, deciding what age to be. Nancy, or rather, Natacha, had been twenty-nine for five years, and, so far, things had gone quite smoothly. Just the odd tricky moment here and there, but nothing of major importance. Moving from her home town to London had of course helped a lot. There was no one in London to remember that she had already been twenty-nine for several years.

The big problem came as a result of the unexpected success of her first novel, *Lovers-in-law*. Not initially, though. Initially things had gone very well indeed. Her lucky break had come through her friend Delia, who happened to be secretary to the editorial director of Pabulum Press Plc.

'If you like I'll take it to my boss,' she said. 'I can't guarantee he'll like it, but at least he'll read it, not just hand it over to an editor's reader, who might not like it.'

'But your boss might not like it either.'

'True, but at least it will be one hurdle less to clear.'

As it happened, Richard Rick did like the novel, and eventually it appeared in an attractive paperback edition. Sales were not astronomical, but perfectly satisfactory. Nancy, or rather Natacha, as she diligently now remembered to call herself, kept thanking her lucky stars that she had been prompted to write up her own earlier love affair. No need to worry over finding a plot! All she had had to do was stick to the facts, with a little embroidery here and there, and, of course, a happy ending. For, as she put it to herself, if fiction can't improve on real life, what's the point.

Another little improvement had been her change of name. Nancy Mulligan had been deemed rather inappropriate for a romantic novelist.

'You want something a little more exotic, with a touch of class to it.' That's what Richard Rick had said, and Nancy had been perfectly willing to agree that Mulligan was neither exotic nor classy. When she had come up with Natacha Maudsley, Richard had nodded thoughtfully.

'Yes . . . yes, that sounds just about right. How do you spell Natacha – "sh" or "ch?"'

'I think "sh" is the usual way. In fact, it's the only way I've ever seen it.'

'Right, then. We'll make it "ch". We don't want to be usual, do we?'

'No, of course not.'

The first cloud to appear on Natacha's horizon came when she realized that Richard expected her to produce another novel in the not too distant future. After that, every time he mentioned the idea, she would tell him earnestly that she was working on it, which, in a sense, she was. But what she was working on was the problem of how to find a plot; not, alas, the novel itself. She had used up the one idea that her own experience had given her, and, try as she would, she simply couldn't find another subject.

She had come to dread hearing Richard's voice on the phone, and knew that, sooner or later she would have to admit that she hadn't even got started on the next novel. And then one day he phoned, and didn't even mention the second novel. He started off by asking her age, which rather surprised her.

'Twenty-nine,' she said, wondering how much longer she could afford to be this age. Not that it showed in her appearance. Oh, no, not that! Simply that people noticed after a while.

'Great!' exclaimed Richard. 'Just the job.'

'I . . . I don't quite understand.'

'Listen. I've decided to enter *Lovers-in-law* for a literary prize.'

'Oh, Richard, how exciting! Tell me more.'

'It's the Pamela Fortune Best Romantic First Novel. How does that grab you?'

'It sounds wonderful. Tell me more.'

'Well, the prize money is ten thousand pounds – '

'Ooh!'

' – and it's for a romantic novel, which yours eminently is, published within the past year, which yours certainly was, as a first novel, which yours most emphatically is, by an author not yet thirty years of age, which, as it turns out, you are – or rather, aren't.'

This last condition of entry had suddenly darkened Natacha's horizon. Not that she minded being entered for a competition on false information. After all, she didn't *feel* over thirty! What worried her was the fear of being found out. There would be the ignominy of being caught cheating, and in addition, everyone would then know her real age. And this was something she felt she simply couldn't risk, especially because of Lance.

For the last three months Natacha and Lance had been living together, and she was very much in love with him. So much in love that she felt the affair might last at least another three months! Perhaps even longer, who knows? Perhaps even long enough for her dream of a happy marriage to come true.

Now, Lance had been told, like everyone else, that she was twenty-nine. As he was only twenty-seven she had felt it would be rather impolitic to reveal her real age. If the truth were now to leak out, she was sure he would write her off completely, not so much on account of her age – she now knew him well enough to realize that this wouldn't really matter to him – but because of the deception she had practised on him and the world at large.

Altogether, it would be utterly disastrous if this competition thing led to an unfortunate revelation. She felt she really couldn't risk it.

She would have to back-pedal.

'It sounds very tempting,' she said, 'But I don't really think I want my book to be entered.'

'Why on earth not?' Richard sounded quite incredulous.

Natacha murmured things about it not being her scene, the novel not being good enough, her own lack of competitiveness, and so on. All rather feeble stuff, she had to admit.

'Nerves, sheer nerves,' was Richard's verdict. 'I'm not going to let you put me off with all this waffle. Think of the glory! Think of the publicity! Think of the *money!*'

'Yes, I know, Richard, it's just . . . ' Her voice trailed away. She couldn't really tell him, could she, that she'd be thrilled to be entered for the competition, provided she could feel sure there was to be no verification regarding her age.

Richard overruled all her objections, and she had to settle down to a few months of mingled emotions – fear of having her deception discovered, and a thrilling little hope that perhaps her novel might win the prize. She had given up all idea of trying to find out whether there was any verification of ages likely to take place, for who could she approach in the matter without giving away her cause for concern? All she could do was wait, and hope for the best.

'We're on course!' Richard's voice sounded friendlier than it had been since he at last discovered the truth about the second novel. He had not been at all pleased to hear it wasn't even in embryo.

'On course, Richard?'

'*Lovers-in-law* has got through to the shortlist. Results to be announced at a dinner on 5th May – which you shall, of course, attend.'

'Oh, Richard, how utterly fantastic! I can hardly believe it!'

Natacha was genuinely thrilled. She assumed that, since things had reached the shortlist stage, there was no longer any danger of any inconvenient questions being asked about her age. There was now nothing to fear, and everything to hope for.

By early May Natacha was in a state of ill-suppressed excitement. Thank goodness Lance was to be there. He would exercise a calming effect on her nerves. Richard, of course, would be there too, but his effect would hardly be calming. He'd really been nagging her about that new novel. He had even insinuated that it was almost immoral for a new writer not to reward her publisher with a second novel in view of the risk he had run in taking on a completely unknown author.

'But I just can't think of a plot!' she had wailed.

'Then go home and rewrite *Romeo and Juliet*. It's been done often enough, so why not once more?'

Natacha had given the matter some serious thought, but was unable to come to a decision for the simple reason that she wasn't quite sure whether he had really meant it. Richard could be quite ironical at times.

Another irony was the fact that she actually *had* thought of a plot: about an author who wins a prize for a novel and is disqualified over a slight inaccuracy about her age! Really quite a good plot. What a pity she couldn't use it!

The great day came, and Natacha, looking her youthful

loveliest and escorted by Lance, arrived at the scene of the long-awaited great occasion. One of the attractions of the evening was the presence of the previous year's winner, a charming woman with long, ash-blonde hair and a confidential manner.

She had quite a cosy chat with Natana.

'Oh, yes, my dear. It really was so exciting! One moment you're nobody, and the next there they all are, milling around you, asking questions – press, television, the lot.'

'Does it get into the press?'

'But of course, my dear. And the nicest thing of all is that they ask you where you were brought up and they contact your local paper, and your school. And my old headmistress even produced a photo of me as a sixth-former . . . '

After that Natacha stopped listening. If anyone contacted her school, she was done for. Sixth-form photograph! For the year 1977! What a give-away that would be! She would be shamed and discredited, the prize taken from her, Lance would walk out on her, all her friends would abandon her . . .

No, she couldn't face it, couldn't risk it.

She hurried off in search of Richard, and found him in the bar.

'Richard, Richard,' she called urgently. 'I want to withdraw! Please withdraw my entry right away.'

'Good God, Natacha, have you gone mad? What ever for?'

'I can't tell you, I don't know, nerves, call it what you like, but I'm not going ahead with this.'

'Listen, baby, you've just got to calm down. You can't back out now! Think of the glory! Think of the publicity! Think of the *money!*'

In the end Richard managed to persuade her that it was

71

too late to back out, and she took her place at table in a state of the most fearful apprehension.

'Cheer up, sweetheart,' said Lance, 'you stand a good chance of winning.'

'Oh, shut up!' she snapped.

'Sorry, darling. I was only being supportive.'

At long, long last the time for the announcement arrived. Natacha was in such a state of utter dread that she could hardly breathe.

' . . . and this year's winner, we are happy to announce, is Edelmira Athelstone!'

Before the applause burst forth, those sitting near to Natacha heard her impassioned exclamation.

'Thank God!' she gasped in her relief.

After the applause had died down, Lance turned to her, bewildered.

'Darling, did you really not want to win?'

'No, I'd have hated it.'

'But why, why ever not, Natacha?'

Natacha shook her head, lost for words. Then she murmured coyly:

'I just don't think I could have survived the publicity.'

7

Just Waiting

Everything would be different now. Anne knew that great things would be required of them all once war was declared. And it was bound to come – today, tomorrow, the next day . . . The solemn words would be spoken, and from that moment they would all lead dedicated lives. All the uncertainties of her adolescence would be transformed into one great, shared purpose. She felt afraid and uplifted.

Next day, after the words had been spoken, after they had lost the last faint hope that war could be averted, she saw her mother's tears with shock and something not far from disapproval. At fifteen she couldn't cope with the expression of a parent's grief; it seemed almost indecent. And besides, there was going to be no place for weakness now. From now on life must be lived heroically.

She would have loved to enrol in one of the women's forces right away, but she was too young. Then it struck her that she could at least play her part in a slightly more humble way.

'Mum,' she said, 'I think I'll leave school and go to work in a munitions factory. They say they want all the women they can get.'

'You'll do no such thing,' said her mother, while her brother Dick, who was about to join his regiment that very day, observed scornfully, 'They want women, not children.'

'I'm fifteen, I can leave school if I want to.'

'You'll do no such thing,' repeated her mother. Then, turning to her husband, who had just come in, she said, 'She won't, will she, Tom? We won't let her.'

'Certainly not!' Then, giving Anne's nearest pigtail a friendly tug, 'What is it we're not going to let you do?' he asked.

The argument raged for some time. Her father, though consistently jocular, was just as determined as his wife. In spite of her teenage sense of mission, Anne lost the argument.

Two years later her wish was granted.

Only, by that time it was no longer what she wanted. She had been about to leave school, and hoped to join one of the women's forces almost at once, when word came that her brother was missing, presumed dead. In the misery that followed she became aware of how much her parents now depended on her, and of how much she still needed them. So, in spite of her feeling that a complete change would probably be the best thing for her, she took a job in the local munitions factory. Often she thought ruefully of her heroic expectations two years ago when she had fought her battle to be allowed to join in the nation's war effort. She was in it now, and a rather boring business it was. Dull work, with uncongenial companions, and a sad home to come back to.

Where was all the glory?

Ichabod, Ichabod, the glory is departed, she mused. Or rather, it never was there, she had only imagined it. Life, she had noticed, had rather a trick of granting wishes once they were no longer what you wanted. The last-but-one wish, that's the one you're granted.

She had a heavy day at the factory, took her share of the shopping, with its eternal queues, helped in the house, and went to bed tired-out every night. And yet

74

her life seemed empty. What she needed was some high purpose.

Or love.

Both eluded her for the next two years. The cinema, her chief mentor and source of entertainment, supplied her endlessly with models of both. And that was as far as it went. She went on seeing the world in a grey mist, at one remove from reality.

Then her friend Brenda invited her to a party, and Anne decided she must buy that coveted blue dress, even though it was rather dear, and meant parting with some of her precious clothes coupons.

When she came home with it her mother was surprised and slightly reproachful.

'But you decided against it last week, dear.'

'Last week I wasn't going to a party.'

'Yes, but only one party. You'll hardly ever wear the thing. And you'll soon need a new winter coat, and where do you think you're going to get the coupons?'

'From you, I expect,' Anne replied as she slipped into the dress. 'Zip me up, there's a dear.'

'Cheek!' said her mother, then caught her breath as the girl turned round to show off the dress. The rich sapphire colour seemed to intensify the blue of her eyes, and the long dark hair falling over her shoulders formed a frame for the perfect oval of her face.

'Yes, you were right to buy it,' admitted her mother. 'That blue . . . it makes you look like a Madonna.'

Anne's mood changed suddenly. Her quiet satisfaction in the dress and what it did for her gave way to a sudden, startled pleasure. The comparison was a solemn thing. The idea of the Madonna carried her far beyond all thought of parties and entertainments, back to the world of dedication that had haunted her and eluded her for the past four years.

That evening she had only been in the room a few minutes when Brenda came over, followed by a young man in RAF uniform.

'Anne, this is my cousin Frank. He insists on meeting you.'

Frank steered her to a seat in a quiet corner.

'Now,' he said earnestly, 'tell me about yourself.'

She had little to say on the subject, and he had much to say on the corresponding theme of his own self, so their conversation flourished. When he was explaining about his work as a pilot she asked whether he went out on bombing raids.

'Oh, yes. That's part of the job.'

'But that must be dangerous!'

'Yes, it is, rather.'

For a moment they looked at each other in silence. His volubility, his too eager desire to impress, faded from him before the consternation in her eyes. The sophisticated manner, the self-assurance, the over-abundant use of RAF slang, all these young man's tricks, fell from him. They sat quietly talking most of the evening.

Ten days later they were engaged, having spent every available moment together. And three days after that he had to go back to his base.

Anne told him she would see him off at the station.

'Darling, you can't. It's the midnight train. I can't have you going home alone at that time of night.'

But she was adamant. This was one point on which she refused to bow to his superior age and experience.

The station looked like a modern version of Dante's hell. Dimly lit, with crowds of lost souls in the form of young men and women, most of them in uniform, surging backwards and forwards, some staggering under huge loads of baggage, shouting, cursing, falling over each other's luggage. A few silent couples were clinging to each other in the midst of the turmoil.

An ironic cheer rang from the crowd when it was announced that the southbound train would be an hour late in arriving.

'Good,' said Frank. 'That gives us an extra hour together.'

She nodded, too intent on holding back the tears to be able to speak.

A drunk sailor sprawling on a bench beside them struggled to his feet and staggered off. Quickly Frank installed the two of them on the seat. A group of recruits sang raucously and intermittently, snatches of this and that, mostly beginnings. 'Wish me luck as you wave me goodbye,' they sang, and the words made a terrible impact on Anne's troubled mind. She had always hated the cheap, fatuous tune; but now the words held an inescapable message for her. 'With a cheer, not a tear, make it gay,' the singers bellowed.

No, she mustn't cry, she mustn't send him off depressed. She knew she couldn't manage a cheer, but she would fight off the tears to the last. She almost wished they hadn't been granted the extra hour in this embodiment of nightmare. They were still together, but the parting weighed so heavily on them that it might as well have taken place already. They could no longer feel joy in each other's presence, lost as they were in the impending misery. They could no longer even speak to each other.

The hour dragged on endlessly. She was appalled at the irony of wishing he were already gone. How could she not want him to stay every possible minute? How could she wish he were gone, knowing how desolate she would be without him? Sadly, she came to realize that parting takes place some time before the physical separation.

When at last the train came in, Frank was swept into it

by the jostling crowd, and was unable to get near enough a window to wave to her, and she was glad, glad, as she turned away and let the tears fall at last. She felt sure she hadn't fooled him; but she had played her part, she hadn't broken down. 'Not a tear . . . ' Not in his presence, anyway.

Now, as the train steamed out of the station, she leaned against a pillar on the suddenly empty platform and burst into passionate sobbing.

From that moment the shadow cast by the war took on a new form – more tragic and more threatening. But at least her sense of emptiness and aimlessness had gone. She had found her lodestar. Waiting became the chief mode of existence for her. Waiting for his next leave, when they were to be married, waiting for his first letter.

It came surprisingly soon. She found it on the hall table when she came in from the factory one evening, and ran up to her bedroom to read it in private. It was perfect. Short – for he had written it the very morning of his arrival at the camp, only a few hours after he had left her – but full of love and longing. He thanked her for being so composed and courageous at their parting. He knew it must have cost her a great effort. At this, the suppressed tears came flooding out again, as if she hadn't already wept them a dozen times since that night.

When she had wiped her tears and washed her face she went back downstairs and sat down beside her father in the living-room.

'Umm,' he said to acknowledge her presence, carefully not looking up from his paper.

Her mother was coming and going, getting the meal ready.

'Frank?' she asked.

Anne nodded.

'That was quick,' smiled Mother.

'Full marks for punctuality,' observed Father. 'How was the spelling?'

'Impeccable. He even spelt my name right.'

'Not bad, not bad,' conceded Father. 'But what about his punctuation?' He put down his paper and looked at Anne with a preposterously solemn face. 'Punctuation! Now, there's a test for you! Can this young man punctuate?'

'Perfectly,' Anne assured him, 'and what's more, he's got lovely handwriting.'

'Oh, we know all about that. Your mother examined that envelope with a magnifying glass. Nothing escaped her.'

The two women laughed.

Anne found herself wondering how she would have reacted if the letter had not come up to the high educational standard the whole family took for granted. After all, she knew so little about him. Less than two weeks of even the most indefatigable self-revelation could hardly fill all the gaps. And suppose he had written 'affect' instead of 'effect', or let his sentences run into each other?

She was astonished at the intensity with which she felt she'd had a narrow escape.

In the end she convinced herself that it was only because she knew her parents would object to an educationally sub-standard son-in-law. And yet . . . She had to admit that it would have been a flaw. And he was flawless, the letter had been perfect.

Perfect.

Letters came and letters went continuously. Twice he announced the date of his next leave, and preparations were made for the wedding, and twice the leave was cancelled. Anne came to think of the war not just as an impersonal cloud of black misery that had descended on them all, but rather as a malignant monster, bent on keeping her and Frank apart. But sooner or later he must get leave, the wedding would take place, and they would move into married quarters at the base. No more letters; his presence instead.

How she longed for this moment to come!

At last the wedding took place, they had a brief honeymoon, and then travelled together to the base, to settle into their first home. She was so happy to be there that none of the disadvantages of the place could touch her. The shabby furnishings, the stained carpets – none of it registered.

'Oh, Frank, we'll be so happy here!'

He left her to go and report. A quarter of an hour later he came back, white-faced and tense. He told her that the very next day he was to be sent abroad.

'I'll come with you. Anywhere, anywhere.'

'You can't. No wives allowed.'

Anne sat and stared at the empty grate for a long time. At last she broke the silence.

'It's the last-but-one wish again, I see.'

'The what?'

'Oh, of course. You don't know.' Once again she thought of all the things they didn't know about each other. Would they ever have time to catch up? She explained that it's always the last-but-one wish that is granted. 'Or that's the way it seems, anyway. I so wanted to be here, I'd spent months longing to be here. And here I am. Only, you're going tomorrow.'

After he had gone she packed her things and took the first train home, back to her parents, back to the factory.

Life resumed its dreary round, dominated as always by the war. She thought of her expectations years ago, when war was declared, and of the excitement and exhilaration she had expected it to bring. So far the only excitement she had felt was the vicarious one of knowing what danger Frank was in. And from his letters it seemed that he wasn't finding life all that exciting and exhilarating either. One long, ghastly grind, was his description. She had to admit that she couldn't call her daily life ghastly, but it certainly was a grind – tiring, frustrating, and desperately boring.

Anne had spent years waiting for heroism to be called for. Gradually it came to her that the form of heroism being demanded of her was simply endurance – a singularly unheroic form of dedication, just working and waiting. Waiting for Frank's next letter, for his next leave.

Waiting in queues.

Waiting for the war to end.

Just waiting.

8

Maria

And it will come, oh yes, it will come, for it *must* come, the time of loving and having and holding. The time when she will run to me, and nestle close, and let me hold and rock her in my arms, and call her mine, mine, mine.

For she *is* mine, she has to be; she is my breath and my very being, the bread I work for, the bread I live by, the wine on my table and the candle at my altar. Her light illumines me, her smile, which I have never seen, is my heavenly hope.

The priest would scold me if he heard these words. My son, you must restrain this passion, check this inordinate desire. This is idolatry. My son, my son . . .

Mumble and grumble, priest, mumble and moan. You can condemn me to the very fires of hell, mumble and grumble and grumble and groan. I live in hell already.

Hell is where she is not. My house is hell, the fields I work in, hell.

I have not heard her voice, I have not seen her smile. I know her name – Maria. I see her in the street – rarely – beside her mother. I see her in the church. My son, my son, your eyes are roaming. Yes, and my heart is roaming, and my mind and my whole spirit. Your Christ has been eclipsed. I pray to her.

I have nothing, I am nothing. Why should she look at me, the son of a poor peasant? And yet, another Mary brought her son into this world for us.

All day I work in the fields, and I come home at nightfall, and I walk through the silent village streets, past her window. Is she there, behind the blind? Does she see me, does she understand why I cannot hurry past her house, why I must linger? Does she know why my footsteps drag outside her window, does she know why I sigh?

Does she as much as know that I exist?

Maria, Maria, you hold me in the palm of your hand. Don't throw me away like a handful of dust!

The priest says, pray, and God will hear your prayer. But I've prayed to God the Father and I've prayed to God the Son. Even the Blessed Virgin will not hear. Who else is there to pray to? The saints? What good are saints, when even God won't listen?

Dear God, give me Maria. Let me speak to her, let me see her smile, let me hear her voice.

My holidays are when I see her, and these are truly holy days for me.

Idolatry, idolatry!

And she walks past, silent, beside her mother, with eyes downcast, always with eyes downcast. The sweet, pure face in the dark cloud of hair, like the image of the Holy Virgin in the church. Maria, Maria! But this one is more beautiful – she is alive. She breathes and walks, and one day she will look at me.

And one day she must look at me. She must, if there is any justice on this earth.

And all the rainbows of the earth will gather round to form her diadem. The birds will sing, the sun will shine, the flowers will pay their tribute in a riot of bright petals at her feet. And all the creeping things beneath the soil will struggle out and upwards to be there, to see her pass, and to be blessed by her sweet smile. The air will be full of the soft beating of wings, for all the tiny birds will come to see and worship her.

She will walk through this procession of praise, silent, unaware. Her look will be for me. She will not see the flowers or rainbows, she will not hear the birds. In her great awakening she will see only me.

But I shall see the glory round her, I shall hear the birds, their long-rehearsed song, the flutter of their wings. I shall feel the gentle caress of the petals as they float down to pave her way. I shall know the ecstasy of the breeze that fondles her cheek, and feel the anguish of the future and the yearning of the past annulled by this imperious now.

Weeks have gone past, and days and months. Weeks of waiting and days of dust and despair. I pray to her all day. I pray to have her, here, beside me, mine. My life is nothing but this long waiting, this infinite, unspoken prayer.

Hosanna!

It has happened! I have looked deep into her eyes, our eyes have met.

Every Sunday, as soon as Mass is over, I step outside and wait at the church door, beside the beggars. That is where I belong, for do I not spend all my life begging for one look from her?

Today I stood as always, on the steps, waiting, watching, praying my profane prayer – Maria, Maria, have mercy upon me!

I saw her mother coming out, and everything stood still, for I knew Maria must follow, with downcast eyes, always with downcast eyes. And as she appeared I held my hand out, like the beggars, only the alms I wanted was one look from her.

And in her mercy she looked up at me, and our eyes met.

There were no petals and no rainbows, and the birds sang

no hymn of praise. Instead, there was a great and holy stillness, an endless silence, while her eyes looked into mine. That second lasted for a hundred years. Nothing will shake it, nothing can break it. It is the rock on which my life can now be built.

9

The Wee Malkie

'Ah want yir money.'

The woman looked at the urchin who had just shot out from the bushes, blocking her path. Her first reaction was one of incredulity. Then she rallied.

'I'm not giving you any money.'

'Ah want yir money.'

'That's no way to ask.'

'Ah'm no asking, Ah'm telling ye.'

The woman tried to push past him, but he side-stepped adroitly, and there he was standing in front of her again, less than two feet away.

The woman decided to change tactics.

'Go away,' she said. 'Shoo!'

This produced a burst of delighted laughter from the boy.

'Ye'll no get rid of me that easy,' he said.

The woman looked along the path behind the boy. It stretched on up the hill for over a hundred yards. Not a soul in sight. She glanced quickly behind her, down towards the park gates a long way below. Nobody there either. Her tormentor was evidently amused by her reconnaissance.

'Naebody there,' he pronounced with satisfaction.

The woman felt humiliated and angry. 'If you don't go away,' she said, 'I'll scream for help.'

'Ye can scream yir heid aff,' said the boy. 'It disnae bother me. See they bushes? Wan scream fae you an' Ah'll be in amang that lot in twa shakes o' a coo's tail. An' Ah'll hae yir money, an' yir braw bag an' a'.'

The woman tightened her hold on her handbag. The boy observed her movement with the practised eye of a connoisseur.

'Haud on tae it,' he said ironically. 'Ye can haud on, but Ah'll hae it aff ye for a' that.' He lowered his head and made as if to butt her. 'Wan dunt in yir belly, an' the last thing ye'll think o' is haudin' on tae yir bag.'

The threat of physical violence brought a nasty little thrill of fear to the woman.

'Sae ye can take yir choice,' the boy went on. 'You gie me the money or Ah take yir bag. An' ye can take yir time to decide. Ah widnae like ye tae make a hasty deceesion. Ah'm in nae hurry, as lang as naebody comes alang. If they dae, Ah've telt ye whit'll happen. You'll be rolling about on the grass wi' a pain in yir peenie, an' Ah'll be awa' into they bushes.'

'You can't stay in the bushes all day. The police will get you.'

The boy gave her a patronizing smile. 'Listen, hen,' he said, 'yous yins is awfie nave – that's a furrin word, means kinnae simple, like. Ye think a' ye've got tae dae is mention the polis an' we'll a' rin awa'. Nae chance,' he concluded with contempt. 'It'd no be the first time an' it'll no be the last.'

With appalled clarity the woman realized that she was entirely in the hands of the little horror in front of her. He had nothing to lose; that was his great strength. Falling into the hands of the police was obviously just an occupational hazard. She tried to work out how old he must be – eleven, twelve? Small and skinny and shabbily dressed, yet he was manifestly her superior in the present confrontation. As if to confirm this realization

87

the boy went on, affably offering a number of suggestions.

'There's a' sorts o' things Ah could dae tae ye. Ah could staun' on yir fine shoes. That 'ud spoil them, and it wudnae dae much for yir corns eether. Or Ah could kick ye in the shins. Ruin yir stoakins, that wud, an' make mincemeat o' yir shinbones. Or Ah could spit on yir posh jaicket.'

Despairingly the woman threw a hasty glance behind her.

'Naw, there's naebody comin'. It's owre cauld. Just you an' me, hen.'

The little brute was right, of course. It was far too cold for the casual walker. For the first time the woman cursed the good circulation that made it a pleasure for her to go out walking when everyone else was sitting huddled over the fire. It was a pleasure and also a matter of pride. Telling her friends how far she had walked in this or that park afforded her a great deal of satisfaction.

'Whit aboot it, missis?' The small, pinched face looked up at her ironically, enjoying the game of pretending the woman had any choice in the matter.

Suddenly the recollection of a poem her son had read out the other night came to her, and crystallized the vague sense of threat in which she had been living for the past few minutes. That's it, she thought, 'The Wee Malkies'. He's one of the wee Malkies. Her son's class had been doing it at school and he had thought it was great. She hadn't understood it, but had hated it thoroughly. All she had got out of it was a sense of powerlessness in the face of an uncontrollable and alien force.

'Whit'll ye dae when the wee Malkies come . . . ?'

That was the beginning. It was the word 'missis' which the urchin had used that had brought the poem back to her in full force. Yes, that was it – 'Haw, missis, whit'll ye dae?'

The fact that she didn't understand it made the poem all the more threatening. What had got through to her was a feeling of the helplessness of being invaded by creatures who are not bound by the rules you live by. Whatever the wee Malkies were, she was convinced she now had one of them in front of her.

The boy was still standing there, arms akimbo, with a sardonic expression on his meagre face.

The recollection of the poem had unnerved her completely.

'How much do you want?' she asked, crumbling.

'That's no the question, hen. The question is, hoo much hae ye got?'

'Five pounds,' she said.

'Come aff it!' he exclaimed. 'Your sort disnae gang aboot wi' nae mair as five pun on them. Ah'm looking for a lot mair as that.'

As it happened, she had forty pounds on her that day, rather more than she usually carried.

'Ten,' she offered.

'Come on, hen, this is no a bluidy auction. See's owre yir bag.'

Utterly cowed, she complied.

'Ye'll get it back,' he assured her amiably.' Ah dinnae want yir credit cairds. Nae use tae me. And no the bag eether. No ma style.'

The first thing he found was the envelope with her name and address on it. She always carried one about, 'in case of accident'. He looked at it critically.

'Hm,' he said, 'no a bad address. Hazel Bank, nae less. Quaite Kelvinsaide, izzit no? Might drop in for a cup of tea, me an' ma chums, wan o' these days.' He made as if to lift a cup to his lips, little finger delicately extended. 'See an' get yir best cheenie oot,' he added.

It didn't take him long to find the bank notes. He pocketed them and then opened the purse. Taking out the few pound coins he handed purse and bag over again.

'Ah've left the chainge in yir purse,' he announced quixotically. 'Pay yir bus fare hame.' Then he nodded and turned away. 'See ya,' he said, as he dived into the bushes.

The woman began walking unsteadily down towards the park gates, feeling as if a huge chasm had opened up in front of her.

Whit'll ye dae when the wee Malkies come?

When, not *if*, she thought, and remembered that the title of the poem was 'The Coming of the Wee Malkies'.

Would this coming, then, take place?

Was she really to expect them?

She had a vision of her well ordered house overrun by the little monster and his chums. Nothing would be safe, nothing would be sacred. She tried to convince herself that he was just joking when he said they would drop in for a cup of tea. The brat obviously had quite a sense of humour. Sick humour, of course, but still . . .

Perhaps after all he didn't really mean to come. Then she thought of his parting words – 'See ya' – and wondered how much weight to attach to them. Was it just a harmless formula, or was it a threat?

Try as she would she couldn't shake off the conviction that life would never be the same again. Security and predictability had disappeared for good. The rules, her rules, no longer applied.

Haw, missis, whit'll ye dae?

10

Only Petal

'Petal?' he said. 'That can't possibly be your real name.'

The girl looked at him with smiling grey eyes. 'Yes, I'm afraid it is. Rather a silly name, isn't it?'

Before looking into those eyes Paul would have agreed entirely. In fact, the name had struck him as utterly ridiculous. But the grey eyes and the delicate features and the flowing golden hair convinced him of his mistake. With complete sincerity he answered, 'It's perfect. Perfect for you. No one else could get away with it.'

Petal smiled at him, accepting his compliment without vanity and without embarrassment. They stood talking for a long time, though afterwards he was never able to remember what they had spoken about. All he knew was that he was standing beside this beautiful young creature, listening to her warm, friendly voice, utterly enthralled by her presence. It seemed incredible that so young a girl could be so poised, so natural, so utterly at home in her world. And he couldn't understand how anyone so resplendently young could want to spend so much time talking to him. Surely she must realize that he was at least twice her age. But it didn't seem to matter, and he soon forgot about the age difference, too absorbed in their conversation to think of anything else.

Suddenly a young man, obviously one of her contemporaries, appeared and dragged her off.

'My dance,' he claimed. 'You promised me this dance.'

Petal smiled at Paul over her shoulder and said, 'See you later.'

Well, he thought, that's it. I don't suppose for one moment she'll come back. I expect she was just being polite.

He started wandering about the room restlessly, still dazed by the encounter with Petal. Several times he saw someone he knew and would have liked to speak to in normal circumstances. Instead he turned away. He just wanted to go on thinking about Petal. He knew it was ridiculous, of course. After all, he was her senior by some twenty-five years.

He was standing staring out of one of the windows when he felt a soft, warm hand sliding into his, and saw Petal standing beside him.

'I'm so glad I've found you!' she said. 'Were you waiting for me? I was afraid you might have gone off with someone else.'

They spent the rest of the evening sitting on the stairs, talking quietly. At one point Petal interrupted herself to say, 'By the way, are you married?'

'Not now. I once was.'

'Divorced?'

'Yes.'

'I'm so glad.'

Paul was shocked and enchanted at the same time. It must be the generation gap, he thought. In my day girls didn't speak like that. No decent girl would have dared to make her feelings so clear. He wondered whether they were all like this now. Or was this extraordinary candour something unique in Petal? Whatever it was, he found it delightful and most refreshing. How guarded we were, he thought, my God, how guarded and suspicious and insincere, when I was Petal's age! He felt as if he'd been transported to a different world, a limpid, clear, translucent world, where everything was pure and straightforward and true.

At the end of the evening, when Petal was about to leave with her brother, Paul took her hands in his and said, 'When can I see you again?'

'Tomorrow?' she suggested.

'At the very latest.'

Everyone tried to dissuade them – his friends, hers, his ex-wife Norma, with whom he remained on friendly terms. About the only people who didn't appear to disapprove of the match were Petal's parents.

'We've always let her do what she wants,' they said, 'and she usually gets it right . . . She just seems to have a talent for doing the right thing.'

So they were married and Paul's life became transformed and transfigured by her radiance. Even giving up his flat in the centre of town seemed a small price to pay for life with Petal. A bungalow in suburbia was perfection itself, with Petal there. Even the drive through the rush hour, morning and evening, seemed bearable, knowing he would find Petal waiting at home. And some evenings he would find her waiting for him outside the office. She often turned shopping into an excuse for going into town, just so that they could drive back together.

He had not been consciously unhappy before meeting Petal. But he realized now that his life had been a dull routine, full of uncertainties and apprehensions. Since meeting Petal the world had become warm and welcoming, and he knew exactly where his place in it was – beside Petal, living in her glow, happy in her happiness. He felt he was becoming as relaxed and trustful as she was. Even the greyest days seemed bathed in golden light.

The clouds came slowly, so tenuously that, looking back,

he was never able to decide when the first of them had appeared. Slowly the world became less luminous. Tiny shadows, small patches of mist – suddenly he noticed that they were there. The joy was no longer continuous. There were moments of dissatisfaction, even of irritation.

He was aghast when he realized the cause. His friends had warned him, Norma had warned him, that after eleven years of living alone he would find it difficult to adjust to having another person there all the time. Not if it's Petal, he thought. It seemed impossible that he could ever have enough of her company, still less too much of it. No. That, he was sure, was certainly not going to be a problem. And now, it appeared, that was precisely the problem. He began to feel, in some subtle way, diminished by the impossibility of ever being alone, and realized for the first time the value of all the solitary hours he had spent after his first marriage had ended.

He needed some time for his personal renewal. Time to spend in whatever way he wanted, without consultation. Above all, time when he could feel he was accountable to no one for what he did or left undone.

And now, of course, he was never alone. All day in the office with people there, then all evening with Petal, all night with Petal. It was delightful, of course, and the thought of not being able to spend most of his time with her was quite unbearable. But still, the fact remained: he was never alone.

But how could he even begin to suggest to her that he wanted some time on his own? She would be hurt, and he couldn't bear to think of hurting Petal in any way. Besides, would she understand? After all, she could be alone most of the day if she wanted to. She probably knew nothing of this need to be alone, having always had the choice. If she wanted company she could go and see a friend; if she wanted to be alone, she had all day at her disposal. She could do as she pleased.

And the fact that he had no choice in the matter began to weigh on him, like some sort of arbitrary injustice.

After struggling with the problem for some weeks he came to the conclusion that the only thing he could do was to cultivate the hours spent in the car as his own private time. Admittedly, driving a car through the rush hour may not be the ideal situation in which to practise meditation and reflection. But at least he was alone, with no-one else to talk to or listen to. He must cultivate the art of giving the necessary attention to his driving, while yet keeping some part of his mind free and unaccountable. Yes, that was it, the very word – *unaccountable*. It seemed to express the very essence of personal freedom.

The saving idea came to him in the office one day, and he felt immense relief at the thought that he had at last found a solution to his problem. Not the perfect solution, of course, but better than nothing.

He left the office eagerly, looking forward to the drive home, to start putting his plan into action, and turned towards the lane that led to the car park.

'Hi!' He heard Petal's voice from the other side of the busy street. For a second he felt chagrin at the thought that he would have to put off his experiment in savouring his solitude while driving. Then he saw Petal, and all his love came flooding back.

She was standing on the pavement opposite, waiting for a break in the traffic to let her cross over. She looked so lovely and so radiant that he dismissed his regrets and blessed her for her unexpected presence.

At last a gap appeared in the traffic, and Petal seized her chance, running out in front of a slow-moving van. What she hadn't seen was the speeding car that shot out from behind the van. It gave her a glancing blow as it dashed past, knocking her down. As she fell, Paul saw her head land on the edge of the pavement, practically at his feet.

Later, at the hospital, he was told that death must have been instantaneous.

For a while he lived in what seemed almost palpable blackness. Petal had been the embodiment of light. Now he felt as if the sun had suffered a total and permanent eclipse.

His grief was made all the more unbearable by his sense of guilt. He had felt he was spending too much of his time with Petal, and this was to be his punishment – no Petal, for ever and ever. Now it seemed impossible that he could have wished for even one second less of her company.

At first he couldn't even speak of this to anyone, it seemed too monstrous an admission. Eventually Norma brought him his first crumb of comfort. She spent a great deal of time with him at this point, talking over the whole relationship.

One day, in her downright manner, she said, 'You realize, of course, that the idyll couldn't possibly have gone on for ever, not at that pitch. Sooner or later one or other of you would have had to come up for air.'

'Which one of us?'

'My guess is that it would have been you.'

'Why me?'

'Because you are at heart a solitary. That's one of the things that went wrong with us, if you remember. You found my way of life too sociable. You needed more of your own company than my tastes or habits allowed for. Right?'

'Right.' Paul sat silent for a while, then he said, 'You've hit the nail on the head, you know.'

'You mean it was happening already?'

'Yes, just beginning.'

'Did you tell her?'

'No, thank God.'

'Oh, I don't know. Perhaps you underestimated her. I think she would have understood. She had a great fund of realism. She accepted things as they are. That's why she was such a happy person.'

'Yes,' he agreed, 'she had a real talent for happiness.

After this conversation Paul felt less guilty about his desire to have some time to himself. But he still had a horrible suspicion that the accident itself might have been provoked by his initial reaction on seeing her just then, when he was counting on having the journey home in his own company. Had she seen, or sensed, the momentary chagrin he had felt, and was this what had made her lose her usual poise? Why had Petal, who naturally and spontaneously got things right, got it all so disastrously wrong on that occasion?

The idea that he might be indirectly responsible for her death was so unbearable that he could speak of this to no-one. Only Petal herself could have assured him that she had not guessed his reaction to her unexpected appearance. So there was no hope of ever being released from this fear. He could see no possibility of absolution.

His friends persuaded him that he must give up the bungalow and go back to his former way of life in the city centre. After all, he had always hated suburban life, and what was the point of wasting an hour, morning and evening, travelling to and from work? Why indeed? he thought. That time might have been put to some use before, while Petal was with him. Now there was no need for that solitary hour. He had plenty of time in his own company, now. So he had a 'For Sale' sign put up in the garden, and began looking for a suitable flat in town.

One evening, sitting alone by the fire, he turned round

suddenly and looked at the room behind him. He was sitting in semi-darkness, with only the light from the reading lamp beside him. He had got the impression that there was a light behind him. Had he left the door open, and was the light from the hall shining in? But no, the door was closed, and there was no light switched on in the room except for his reading lamp. He decided he must be getting tired and that it was time for bed. Or perhaps he ought to see about his eyes.

Two days later the same thing happened again. After that it became fairly frequent. Eventually he was able to see that there was indeed a faint light, more like a quiet glow, shining intermittently in different parts of the house. At first it faded away almost as soon as he looked directly at it. With practice he was able to hold on to it longer. And every time it came he felt a sensation of peace flooding over him, comforting him. He would have liked to tell someone else about it – Petal's parents, for instance. Perhaps they too would be comforted. But he felt sure no-one would believe him. They would all think his grief had deranged him. Perhaps, he thought, perhaps it's just something purely subjective. He didn't want to be talked out of his comfort by the voice of reason.

Norma came to see him one evening and greeted him with the words, 'So you've sold it? I see the sign's gone.'

'Yes, it's gone, but I've not sold the house. I've decided to stay here.'

She couldn't believe him, especially as he would give no concrete reason for his change of plan. They sat and discussed it for a long time, while she tried to persuade him to sell the house and move out, and he kept affirming that he wanted to stay.

At last, to cut short the argument, he went to make some coffee.

After a minute Norma came running into the kitchen, looking pale and upset.

'Norma, what ever's the matter? You look frightened.'

'I've just seen something very strange. Uncanny. A light appeared in the room, and there was no light to cause it – I mean no lamp, nothing.'

'So!' he exclaimed. 'You've seen it too. This is very, very interesting. So it's not just a figment of my imagination.'

'But what is it, Paul, what on earth is it?' Norma looked really shaken.

Paul put his hands on her shoulders reassuringly. 'It's all right, Norma, nothing to worry about. Just the opposite, in fact. It's Petal, bless her. Only Petal. Nothing to worry about,' he repeated. 'Nothing, nothing at all.'

11

The Vineyards of the Priorat

'You'll do as I say.'

'Yes, Father.' Bernat answered in a dead, expressionless voice.

Yes, Father; yes, Father; yes . . . That's my whole life, as it's been since childhood, as it will be till this man dies. And he's not yet fifty, and strong as an ox. By the time he dies I'll be middle-aged, perhaps even old. And I'll have spent my whole life saying:

'Yes, Father. Yes . . . '

When he dies, I'll be master. Master of Can Carrera, of whatever may be left of it, by that time. Till then, I'm his slave. Like my mother, another slave. And Can Carrera can slowly crumble to dust, for all he cares.

Bernat picked up his trowel and went off to the part of their property his father had decided he was to work in that day. He trudged along till he came to the chosen field, and then started working furiously, spurred on by his anger. As he worked he visualized the family dwelling. He saw the simple yet noble outline of the eighteenth-century *masia*, with the arched entrance in the gable wall, and the smaller arches of the gallery running along the side of the building one floor up. He saw the big, low-ceilinged hall that the huge doors opened on to, with its strings of tomatoes and onions hanging from the beams. Working out there in the blazing sun, he could almost feel the coolness of the long, dim room, lit only by the open doorway.

This was where the family lived on working days, where they took their meals, sitting by the open door in summer, and deep inside the room, beside the blazing fire, in winter. Beyond were the kitchen, the dining-room and the *saló*, but these last two were never used except on feast days. And upstairs, the long gallery leading to all the bedrooms.

It had been an aristocratic house in its day, and the property was prosperous enough to sustain a less austere lifestyle than theirs. But the financial situation wasn't the problem. Grau Carrera's negative attitude to the place was what lay at the root of the trouble. Bernat had been told the whole sad story by his mother, and realized that nothing was going to change his father's attitude.

For what the owner felt for Can Carrera was not indifference, but hatred. In his youth Grau had wanted to go to Barcelona to study law; but his father had insisted that the eldest son, *l'hereu*, had to stay at home and take over from his father when the time came, so that he in his turn should hand it over to his eldest son. Grau, whose inclination found nothing to satisfy it in country life, had lacked the courage to defy his father. He had grudgingly stayed at home, and just as reluctantly had taken over the whole concern on his father's death. And he had taken his revenge by running the place as badly as possible, as if he were determined to destroy it.

But it's my patrimony he's destroying! He wants to leave nothing when he's gone. Nothing for me, nothing for my mother. He has no sense of family, no sense of history, no feeling for the earth. He doesn't deserve to be master of Can Carrera.

Bernat laid down his hoe and straightened out, to stretch his back. Behind him the ground sloped gently down to the dry river bed he had crossed to get here, and beyond that the vineyards rose to a near horizon, crowned by the *masia*. In front of him the ground also sloped gently upwards, to the top of the hill, and beyond that rose another hill, and yet another, all covered with vines.

Near him he could see the green of the vine leaves against the pale, granitic soil. But in the distance the vines seemed to cluster together, covering every inch of the hills with their thick, green velvet. Range after range of hills, with the green getting darker and acquiring a bluish haze on the furthermost range, seen against the vivid blue of the sky. Further to the left, in the distance, the strong hue of the vines gave way to a paler, greyer green. That was where the olive groves began.

As his eyes wandered over this familiar landscape, Bernat gave a great sigh of content mingled with longing. This was his country, his beloved Priorat, and he wanted to play his part in keeping the land fertile and in maintaining the lordly *masies*, with their traditions and history. He was a part of all this, and it depended on him.

But what can I do, what can I ever do, with him always in the way, with him bent on destroying it all?

As if in answer, he seemed to see his father standing in his favourite spot in the courtyard, leaning over the parapet of the well, looking down into its dark water. With a sense of shock Bernat stooped and, picking up his trowel, began working again, as if to clear his mind of the image that had flashed before it.

Yes, there he stands beside the well, leaning over, looking down. It would be so easy. All I'd have to do is walk past, or rather, look as if I was going to walk past; and then, when I'm behind him, one quick, resolute movement . . . I grab his legs, tip him over . . . There's a lot of water in the well, after all the winter rain. And it's deep, very deep. Even if he didn't get killed by the fall, he would drown. There's nothing he could climb up by. No footholds; nothing.

Well, I'm not thinking of that. I'm going to forget it. It's not what I want, it's not anything I could even think of doing. Forget it, get on with the work. Just a wicked, crazy image that came into my mind. I don't know how it got there. The devil must have conjured it up.

For a while he worked hard, trying to forget the disturbing image, shocked that it had even flashed briefly into his consciousness.

That's not the answer, anyway. It would be murder, parricide. I can't even consider it. No, I can't consider it, even though it would be the answer to all our problems. I could save the building, look after the land as it deserves. And I could marry – I'm sure Mariona of Can Coll would have me. And my mother's very fond of Mariona, so there would be no problem there.

Can Carrera would recover its place in the world, and the land would prosper, and the vines would yield their grapes and the grapes would yield their wine, the famous *vi del Priorat*.

And this is what my sons would inherit, and their sons after them. And this is what would be, if it weren't for him.

It would be so simple, but dangerously simple. For a man doesn't disappear, just like that, without anyone noticing. People would ask, 'Where's your father?' and what would I say? Tell me that, just what would I say?

Yes, the real problem would be explaining away his disappearance. And perhaps I wouldn't be able to inherit till he had been proved dead.

It's not so simple, is it?

But a voice inside him kept telling him it was simple, beautifully simple.

All right, yes, it would be simple, the act itself would be simple. But afterwards, what about afterwards? How do we explain my father's absence? Just tell me that.

And yet, it could be done, it can be done. It's just a matter of not complicating things.

Suppose my father were to get a dizzy turn one day, when he's looking into the well. He would fall in, wouldn't he? Or, at least, he *might* fall in. Then what? We hear him yell, don't we? And I come running out of the stable, and my mother comes running out of the kitchen, and we meet in the yard.

'What was that, Bernat?'

'I don't know. I heard a yell, that's all.'

'Where's your father?'

'I don't know.' I don't know anything, do I? 'He was here, coming out of the house when I went into the stable just now. Did he say where he was going?'

'No, he said nothing. But you know where he always goes after supper, just stands at the well . . . '

And then we exchange a horrified glance and run to the well, and look down. But it's too dark to see anything. So I hurry off to get a torch.

When I get back my mother is standing there, looking very tense. What is it that's making her look so pale and shaken? Fear? Hope? Does she sense her release is at hand?

The well is so deep that the beam from the torch only lights the water at the bottom very faintly. Enough, though. Enough to see a huddled body floating on the dark water. Enough to see the bright red of the *faixa*. For my father is one of the very few *pagesos* who still wears the traditional *faixa* wound round the waist.

It's nearly dark by now. Nobody left working in any of the vineyards.

'Where can we get help?' My mother's question sounds absurdly urgent. Is she playing the part she knows she has to play? Or is she really concerned?

'I'll saddle the horse and ride to the village. We can't get him up without help.'

And that's it. Perfectly straightforward. I come back with the men and their ropes and pulleys, and eventually we get the body up, just as the local doctor appears, for someone in the village has sent for him.

And yes, he's dead, nothing to be done.

Then the questions, of course.

There would be no problem about him standing beside the well, everybody knew that was his habit. But why did he fall in? And someone asks, do we think it was suicide? And we both deny it indignantly. And then I mention the fact that he'd had a dizzy turn a few days before, and my mother confirms this.

'But he refused to see the doctor about it. You know what Grau was like.'

And in the end they all agree, doctor included, that he must have taken a dizzy turn while he was leaning over the well, looking down at the water.

Accidental death, that would be the verdict. And a nice funeral. And that would be the end of it.

And then, after the funeral, my life will begin, my real life. And Can Carrera will gradually recover its old splendour. I'll have the house repaired, and the stables. I'll buy new vines, I'll get more help, buy a new horse. All the things that need to get done will be seen to. Instead of living in the midst of decay and abandon we'll see the property begin to flourish again, and Can Carrera will take its place once again among the distinguished names of the Priorat.

And I'll walk through these vineyards and see nothing but health and growth. I'll see the first leaves appearing, and then the tiny, hard green grapes, so small and sparse that they look as if they could never mature into the opulent bunches that weigh the branches down. And all my forefathers will look down on these fields and bless them. And they will thank me for having brought new life to the beloved land, for having upheld the old traditions. And, in years to come, my descendants will tell of how the whole place was allowed to go to rack and ruin, and of how it was saved by the hard work and good sense of one man. They will remember how Grau Carrera nearly ruined the whole property, and how his son Bernat put things to rights. But they will never, never know how much they will really owe me.

When he got back to the courtyard he saw his father standing beside the well, looking down into its depths, as usual. As Bernat approached, his father spoke to him, without raising his eyes from the water that seemed to hypnotize him.

'Go and get the pig out of the vegetable patch. It's got out again.'

Of course it's got out again! The whole pigsty's falling to pieces.

'And hurry up about it, or there'll be no cabbages left.'

'Yes, Father.'

For days he thought about the tempting plan, and asked himself whether he'd ever have the courage to put it into operation. At times the project seemed so simple, so foolproof, that he wondered why he could possibly hesitate. At other times he felt a sense of panic, as he realized he could never be absolutely sure that nothing would go wrong. And what then? What if he didn't manage to throw his father into the well? What sort of punishment could you expect from a father who knows his son has just tried to kill him? Even if he did succeed in killing him, how could he be sure there would be no tell-tale clue to fasten the guilt on him?

And sometimes his doubts were of a different variety. As a practising Catholic he knew that one of the worst aspects of murder is that you send your victim off to his fate with no opportunity to confess his sins and repent. Now, he wasn't really all that concerned about the state of his father's soul. His father was a selfish, wicked, impious man, with no respect for the traditions in which he had been brought up. If he died unshriven, that was no more than he deserved. What worried Bernat was his own spiritual standing if such a situation arose. He didn't really mind if his father ended up in hell. But to be held responsible for sending someone else to this fate, especially for condemning a father to it, that was another matter altogether.

What if he too ended up in hell?

Beside his father, perhaps? That would surely be a fitting punishment.

Bernat took his religion seriously, as did his mother.

As he considered the advantages of getting his father out of the way, one of the aspects that most appealed to him was the idea of being able to marry Mariona of Can Coll. He had admired the girl for a long time, but had always known that, even if his father decided to let him marry, he would never be allowed to pick a bride for himself. And anyway, Grau Carrera had no desire to see his line perpetuated.

But Bernat found himself thinking more and more about Mariona. The following Sunday after hearing mass, as the people stood about in groups in the church square, he walked over to two of his friends and stood talking to them. In a moment three of the girls, Mariona among them, came out and joined the group. The young people formed a little circle as they stood chatting.

Bernat and Mariona were opposite each other. He looked across at her and found her looking at him. It was as if some invisible thread were joining them. A tenuous vibration seemed to hover between them. And the other young people, who were doing all the talking, were left outside this electric current.

Soon the circle broke up, and they all set off, sauntering along the street that led from the church, slowly, at ease, laughing and joking. Bernat and Mariona followed them in silence. Bernat was struck by the way she had allowed him to take his place beside her. They walked on without speaking a word, deeply conscious of each other, slowly, to let their other, noisier companions outstrip them. And even after the others were well ahead, still they said nothing. And yet Bernat felt he had never been so close to anyone in his life, and was convinced that Mariona felt the same.

When it was time to turn back Bernat spoke at last.

'You know what my father's like, don't you, Mariona? A hard and difficult man.'

'Yes, Bernat, I know. We all know.'

'Oh, Mariona, how I wish I could ask you to marry me!'

Mariona looked at him, and nodded gravely.

'But what can I do? You know how things are. What can I do?'

By now they had got back to the church square, and Mariona's parents, who had been talking to another couple, beckoned to her.

'I'm coming,' she called to them. Then, just before leaving him, she turned to Bernat and said, very quietly, 'You can change things.'

And she ran off to join her parents.

Bernat's mother was sitting in the trap, waiting for him to come and drive them home. The father never came to church, so mother and son always had only each other's company during the journey, but they never had very much to say to each other. Dolors was so imbued with the tradition of female silence and obedience that she tended to say little in the presence of her men-folk. And, at twenty-five, Bernat must be treated with the respect due to a man. If he didn't feel like talking it was not for his mother to ignore his wishes.

Bernat sat in silence, trying to puzzle out what Mariona could have meant by her, 'You can change things.' Had she guessed what was on his mind? If so, she seemed to be giving her consent to the undertaking. What else, after all, could she mean? How could he ever change things while his father was still about, still unshakeably in command?

Mariona's words had turned his hesitating design into firm resolve. At the earliest opportunity he was going to take his destiny into his own hands.

Every evening after supper Grau would go out and stand beside the well as usual. At this time of year the sun had just set, but it would be light enough for a long time yet. All the *mossos* would have left the courtyard, and there would be no-one about except his mother, busy clearing things up in the kitchen. This would surely be the ideal time. All he had to do was find some excuse for crossing the yard, and that would be easy enough to find.

Tonight, this evening, tonight I'll do it, I must do it. It must be tonight, for I can't go on living with this thing hanging over me.

Yes, tonight.

He was feeling so tense by supper time that he was almost unable to eat. He forced himself to swallow the food, unwilling to attract attention to himself in any way. He had a strange, quaking feeling inside him, and looked at his hands to see if they were shaking visibly. But they looked perfectly normal.

After the meal was over Grau stood up and went out to the well, and his wife began clearing the table.

Now. *Now* is the moment for action. The moment when

you become a free man. The moment when you become a murderer. No, not that. It's the moment of justice, the moment of righting a great wrong.

Muttering something to his mother about going to see one of the mules that had hurt its leg he went out and began crossing the courtyard obliquely, as if heading for the stables.

Grau must have heard him, as he stood looking down into the blackness of the well, for, just as Bernat dived down to grasp his father's legs, the man swung round suddenly, and delivered a ferocious kick at his crouching son.

Bernat was flung a few yards along the flagstones. His father's kick had landed on Bernat's jaw, making him bite his lip, which he discovered was bleeding profusely when he sat up.

Not a word had been spoken by either man. Bernat was so astonished by the speed with which his carefully laid plan had gone astray that he just sat there, mopping up the blood with his handkerchief.

'What were you trying to do? Throw me into the well?'

'No, of course not.'

'Well, what were you doing, crouching behind me like that?'

'I fell. I was crossing over to see the mule with the damaged leg, and I tripped and fell, that's all.'

Grau looked at his son with the deepest contempt.

'Useless, that's what you are. No good for anything. Go and get your mother to mop you up, you big baby.'

Bernat stood up and walked unsteadily into the house.

'*Verge Santíssima!*' exclaimed his mother, seeing her son's blood-stained face. 'What's happened?'

'I fell.'

'I kicked him.' Grau had followed Bernat into the house.

'You kicked him? You kicked your own son in the face?'

'I thought he was going to throw me into the well. I had to defend myself, didn't I?'

'But what made you think he was going to throw you into the well? For God's sake, what put that idea into your head? Your own son!'

'Well, I didn't know who it was. I just heard someone coming up behind me, and turned round to see him diving at my feet. So I kicked him.'

'Bernat, what happened?' His mother turned her anguished eyes on him.

'I *fell*, I tell you. That's all.'

'Yes, he fell. That's what he says, anyway.'

With a contemptuous look at his son Grau left the house and stationed himself once more at his place beside the well.

'Here, sit down, I'll bathe that cut for you.'

Bernat obeyed his mother and sat down, resting his elbow on the table.

She worked in silence for a moment, then she gave a great sigh and said, 'You're so like your father!'

'Like my father! You think I'm like *him!*'

Dolors nodded and sighed again.

I hate this man so much that I've just tried to kill him, and now she tells me I'm *like* him! Has the woman gone mad?

Mastering his sense of outrage, he asked, 'In what way am I like him?'

His mother said nothing, as if considering she had already said too much.

'Tell me! I must know in what way I'm supposed to be like that man. It certainly isn't in appearance. I'm like you, not him.'

'No, you don't look like him. But you're acting in just

111

the same way. Behaving as if you really wanted to ruin your life.'

'But I want the very opposite of what he wanted! How can you say I'm acting in the same way?'

'Because you're behaving like a coward, just like he did. He was too scared to go against his father's wishes, and he's spent the rest of his life regretting it, and making us pay for it. You're doing exactly the same. You're letting him ruin Can Carrera and all it stands for. He's doing his best to destroy it, but you can change things.'

Bernat looked up, startled. The very words Mariona had used!

Dolors went on, gathering confidence now that she had at last found the courage to speak her mind.

'I know a son is supposed to obey his father in everything, and you've been a dutiful son in that respect. But you also have a duty to the family and its tradition. It's up to you to prevent Can Carrera from falling to pieces. And that means standing up to your father. And I'm not the only one who thinks like this.'

'Who else?'

'Last week I went to Can Coll's, and Ventureta was saying the same thing. So was Mariona.'

So that's the sort of change Mariona meant! I should have known she wasn't thinking of . . . the other thing. I don't need to murder the brute. All I need to do is stand up to him. Easy, isn't it? Just stand up to this bully, with all the authority of the patriarch behind him!

Grimly he reflected that killing the man would have required much less effort and courage. Quicker and simpler, it would have been. And then he thought of his failed attempt, and decided it might not be so simple. But the long, endless struggle against his father seemed something very fearsome indeed.

112

As if she were reading his thoughts, his mother added. 'And you know you'd have me behind you. And the folk at Can Coll. Especially Mariona.'

Bernat spent a restless night, shaken over his failed murder attempt, and in an utter panic at the thought of standing up to his father.

How will I ever find the courage to disobey him? And where do I start?

By morning he had decided where to start – the stable roof, of course. It had been a bone of contention between them for a long time. It seemed symbolic to begin there.

In spite of his sleepless night he was up at the usual time, waiting for his father in the courtyard, with the tools he would need for the job assembled at his feet.

Mariona, Mariona would approve. And my mother will know, and she'll be on my side, even if she doesn't dare to say a word. And once this first moment of disobedience is over it will never be so bad again. I wish you could see me now, Mariona. I think you'd be proud of me.

Grau appeared, glanced at his son, went over to the well, and stood with his back to Bernat, almost defiantly. Without looking round, he said, 'You're to go to the village. I need some rope. You know what kind to get.'

Bernat stooped and picked up his tools.

'I'm not going to the village,' he said. 'I'm going to mend the stable roof. That's more urgent.'

'You'll do as I say,' roared Grau.

Bernat walked on in silence. 'The rope can wait,' he called back over his shoulder.

He climbed on to the stable roof and looked down into the courtyard. His father was standing motionless by the well, glaring at his son, ready to explode again.

Bernat looked down at the handsome, venerable *masia*. Then he let his eyes roam beyond the building, out over the green velvet hills as they rose gently, range after range. In that impressive context, the figure standing by the well looked almost ridiculously insignificant.

12

Fey

The child's fey.

At first the light was huge. It filled the sky, it filled the earth. Heaven and hell were light, full of light. The air was light, the trees and the houses and the hills floated in a mist of light, radiant, luminous. Even the darkness, even the darkness was just a different shade of light. Inextinguishable.

And yet the light was extinguished, defeated.

But it happened slowly, with cunning.

The child's fey.

Slowly, the light acquired boundaries. But it was still huge, enormous. And circular, of course. What other shape could the light take on? A circle, then; huge, immeasurable. But a circle. With bounds. Contained radiance. Contained.

God, or the devils, tightened the circle. The iron hoop pressed tighter and tighter. Inside, the light; still the light. Outside, the iron ring. Black iron. Nothing but black iron, an infinite extension of it, surrounding the light. The circle.

The child's fey.

The iron ring presses tighter and tighter. Everything is now this black iron, with the ring of radiance in the centre. The world a huge black tunnel, with the circle of light at the far end. Smaller, getting smaller, so that you could now cover the light completely with one hand. Smaller still, a pin head.

Smaller. A pin point.

Smaller.

Nothing.

The child's fey, I tell you, she's fey.

Well, I'm not a child any more. I don't have these odd notions now. I see things just as other people see them. As they are. There's light and there's darkness. And sometimes they meet, and sometimes they merge. And they're equally balanced. Neither wins. Which means that neither loses. Good, isn't it? Reassuring. Balance, that's the thing. Balance.

All I have to do if I want more light is close my eyes. Just like anyone else.

Just like anyone else, I've found love. And love has found me. And the light in his eyes is greater than I have ever seen. The light in Adam's eyes. Greater than the huge, unbounded light of my childhood.

On summer evenings we sit by the side of the stream. My mother watches from the window. My mother likes Adam, she knows it's all right. But still, it's her job to watch. So there aren't many kisses. But the kisses will come later, when we're married.

'Tell me, Lizzie, how much do you love me?'

'Count the pebbles in the bed of the stream.'

'But I can't Lizzie. There are too many.'

'Well, that's my love. Beyond counting. Like the pebbles. My love is the pebbles.'

'Oh, Lizzie, you say such strange things. How can your love be the pebbles?'

'Beyond counting. And the water runs over them, for ever and for ever. And they stay there. Also for ever. Nothing will move them.'

'Flood water will move them.'

'There must be no floods. Adam, do you hear? I'll not have any floods.'

'Lizzie, Lizzie, what have I said? Lizzie, why are you crying?'

I told him I would have no floods, but the floods came all the same. They didn't move my love, not one pebble. But they brought this mermaid, this foreign woman with her long golden hair, a circle of light round her head it was, and she dazzled all the men in the village, and I could see her light reflected in Adam's eyes. And he still sat beside me in the evenings, but he sighed, and I knew he was thinking of her. I could see her light in his eyes. Oh, it was her light all right, not Adam's own. How should I not know the difference? This light that was looking somewhere else, not at me at all. The fires of hell were in that light.

I knew when he started kissing her. She had no mother to watch over her, she could do as she pleased. And it pleased her to take my man and drive him mad with the longing for her. I could see it in his eyes, I could feel her kisses hovering round him, like a small trembling animal.

I bore it till I could stand it no longer. And then one day I got up very early, took my mother's two baskets and went down to the river. I stood in the ice-cold water and it said, Yes, yes, take my pebbles, take them, they are yours. And I scooped them up in my hands, two basketfuls of them, and I carried them up the bank, wet and heavy and hard and pure, and I walked along the sleeping street to her house.

I knew where she slept, I knew exactly where her bed was. And because it was summer the window was wide open.

I took a handful of pebbles and threw them in with all the fury of my love, into the corner where the bed was. And the screaming started right away, but I kept on throwing. And when I saw the men running along the street I took the second basket and flung all its pebbles onto the bed. And the screaming went on. I could hear it as the men dragged me along the street.

The mermaid was covered in small, dark bruises, but that was all. It was Adam who lost an eye. One of the pebbles.

After they set me free I went down to the river to the place where I'd scooped out the pebbles. And you couldn't tell, you simply couldn't tell. The bed was flat and even. Not a pebble missing, you'd have said. I sat there for a long time, brooding over the mystery, wondering what it meant. How long had it taken the river to fill up the hollow with new pebbles? Is there no permanence?

I felt betrayed. The river had filled up the hollow as if my action had never been. It had annihilated me. It had flattened, defeated my revenge. For what was left of my fierce fury's storm? The river bed filled up again, the mermaid's bruises mended long ago. Adam's blind eye, that's all that's left.

She's mad, they say. Keep clear of her, she's dangerous. She told great tales about the light, when she was young. But now she's seen the dark. She's singing to it all the time. Hush, can you hear her?

Lighten our darkness, darken our light.
Give us not daylight, but infinite night.
Darken our sorrows and blacken our grief.
Yes, blacken our grief.
Let the dark radiance of hell never cease.
Trouble the desolate, shatter their peace.
Show forth the triumph of pitiless night.
Yes, pitiless night.

118

That's how it is, that's how it has to be. Dark and desolate and pitiless. And it's better that way, don't tell me it isn't better that way. Can't you see the comfort of it?

The comfort of having nothing to lose.

13

Alien Corn

'And that's Mona, the grey one in the corner over there.'

'Grey? That's unusual, surely?'

'Yes, you don't get many like that.' There was just a touch of pride in Jenny's voice. 'She's different.'

Mona turned her head to look at the newcomer. Helen saw the enormous velvety eyes fixed on her, gazing at her in bovine calm. Flattered, almost moved by the long, soft gaze, she put out a hand and laid it on the animal's shining flank.

'She's lovely, she really is lovely.'

Mona gave a huge contented sigh, and turned back to her feed.

'Yes, she's a nice cow.' Jenny sounded matter-of-fact, as if to say it wasn't the thing to get emotionally involved with the animals. Then she added, with an edge of partisanship in her voice all the same, 'But the others are all right too, you know. They're a good bunch.'

'Yes, it's a beautiful herd.'

And that was the beginning of Helen's friendship with Jenny and with Mona.

As a newcomer to the farm she depended entirely on her fellow-worker Jenny for information of all sorts. A year in the Land Army had opened up new worlds to her, and she could hold her own in a conversation relating to field work, crop rotation and the like. But she was new to dairying. And, besides, Jenny had spent all her life on this particular farm, so she could tell you everything worth knowing about farming in general and this farm in particular – how to get the milk cooler to work, where to get the best cow cake, how to groom a fractious young cow, when not to ask the boss for a day off. Jenny knew it all, and was happy to impart her wisdom to her new friend and helper.

'I don't suppose you've learned to milk, then, if you've done nothing but field work.'

'Well, yes, sort of. There were two cows at the farm I was at, and I wanted to learn. But it wasn't my job, so I've done very little. I'm terribly slow.'

'You'll soon pick up speed.'

Jenny's quiet, friendly optimism filled the new girl with confidence and, at the same time, with just a touch of envy. How did one get to be like that? Relaxed, optimistic, gentle. Perhaps a lifetime on the farm did it. The slow pace of life in touch with natural rhythms, the seasons, the animals . . . Then she thought of what life had been like at the last farm, and discarded her hypothesis.

And no doubt there were disadvantages to being Jenny. She looked at the girl's blunt and homely features, her straggling, fairish hair, her stocky figure. She did have nice blue eyes, though. And the nicest thing about them was their expression – peaceful and friendly, and yet with a twinkle. Being Jenny was evidently no bad thing. She was a contented being. Helen reflected ruefully that this was more than she could say for herself.

Soon she plucked up enough courage to ask about the farmer, Mr Morton.

'Is he nice?'

'Yes, he's very nice. But I thought you'd already met him.'

'Yes, but only just. I was just wondering what he's like to work for.'

'Oh, *he's* all right. Some bosses aren't, I know.'

121

Helen smiled, as she took in the fact that Jenny's good nature was prepared to concede that much to the wickedness of the world; and she wondered whether Jenny had heard something about her own recent problems.

'Yes,' she agreed noncommittally, 'some bosses aren't.'

It was a joy to escort the cows back to their field after the milking. Summer was on its way, the air was mild and full of promise. Helen looked with delight at the green of the steep little hills, all crowding together in what really seemed too small a space. She had never seen such a tightly packed landscape, and it filled her with joy and laughter. All those hills, all those dear little hills, nudging each other out of the way, competing for what little space there was. After her spell in the desolate flatness of her last billet, this ebullient landscape delighted her.

They climbed the track slowly, followed by the sound of eighty hooves on the stony ground. It was a comfortable sound – the irregular click-click of hoof on stone, accompanied by the swishing of tails and the gusty breaths of the animals as they climbed the steep slope.

Jenny opened the gate into an almost vertical field, and the girls stood one on each side of the open gateway, ready to shoo in any recalcitrant cow. But the animals followed their leader, docile and untroubled.

After this Jenny took Helen along to the dairy – 'my dairy', as she called it. It took a long time to get everything as spotlessly clean and mercilessly tidy as Jenny required. Before leaving she stopped in the doorway and gave one last, satisfied glance at her domain.

The whole array of gleaming metal utensils hanging against the whitewashed walls or resting on the marble slabs gave a look of order and repose to the place. For the first time in her life, Helen realized the beauty of orderliness. It spoke of peace and repose and readiness for action. But the power of the concrete world wasn't enough to subdue her lifelong habit of seeking out the consecrated words, the fitting quotation for every experience. 'God's in his heaven – all's right with the world!' she thought with satisfaction.

Leaving Jenny at the door of her father's cottage she started the long climb over the shoulder of the hill and across the little patch of moorland to the cottage where she was billeted.

In the evening, after an excellent meal, she sat by the fire with a cat on her lap, and tried to classify the day's impressions. It was odd, this feeling of peace mingled with the excitement of the new. Here she was, less than thirty miles from her last place, and yet in such a different world. All these bumpy little Galloway hills, instead of that depressing extension of arable land, flat and bleak and windy.

Nothing arable here, she thought. You'd have a job finding a field flat enough to plough. But it's not just the scenery. It's the whole atmosphere of the place – the people above all. They're friendly and civilized, they treat you like a human being. And that makes a change!

And indeed it did. That night in bed, as she lay trying to concentrate on the perfections of this new place, the miseries of the old one came back and took hold of her. Try as she would, she couldn't shake off the memory of the long, back-breaking hours spent working alone in a field, the constant cold and constant hunger and, above all, the hostility with which she was treated. Just because she was different. Just because she came from the city and had a middle-class background. So they knew right away that she must be a snob! And nothing she could say or do had improved things. For, as the farmer himself had said to her in one of his more affable moments, 'When all's said and done, in the long run you have to admit you'll never be like one of us.'

And that was as near to any form of conversation as they had ever come. In the end her health had broken down and she'd been sent home to recover.

And now here she was, in this wonderful place, with all these wonderful people. But her Cold Comfort Farm haunted her all night, and for many days and nights to come. No, they couldn't get at her any longer, she had shaken them off. But what she was unable to shake off was the consciousness of her own failure. She hadn't been able to stand the cold and hunger and exhaustion and, above all, the coarseness and unkindness and active hostility. Yet there was a war on, and people were dying, while others were hanging on in the midst of the most terrible hardships.

Well, it was her failure, and she would have to live with it.

And living with it wasn't so very bad after all during the day, working with Jenny and the animals. Soon she knew each cow by name, and which stall it belonged to.

'Do they never get into the wrong stall?' she asked.

'Just occasionally. And it causes quite a commotion, I can tell you. It's quite a job backing her out, with all the others pushing in from behind, in a hurry to get fed. But it doesn't happen often. They're canny beasts.'

Helen got her bucket of warm water and started washing down udders. Jenny started at the other end of the byre and they met in the middle – after a few days, that is. At first they met near the end where Helen had started with Mona. But she soon picked up speed and was able to hold her own.

She discovered that washing a cow's udder is no easy task. It's soft and spongy and very difficult to reach. Either you have to squat down beside the cow, as if you were going to milk her, only without a stool to sit on, or you bend over, with your shoulder wedged into the cow's flank, keeping your feet well apart to give you a steady base, just in case she moves over. This was the position Helen finally decided as best. Mona too seemed to approve, as she would turn her head and assiduously start licking the part of land-girl that was offered to her. Helen got quite used to emerging from the operation with a wet patch on the seat of her dungarees.

She might not have been quite so happy about the cow's reaction with any of the others. Old Jean, for instance. She had quite a temper, and might well have tried taking a nibble instead of just a friendly lick. And Belle! Dear Belle was so exuberant that one friendly lick would have sent you flying into the gutter. But with Mona it was all right. Mona was different. She was special. Helen never managed to work out why she felt like this about Mona. For some reason that she couldn't fathom she sensed there was a bond between them.

Sometimes Jenny's mother would ask Helen in to tea before the evening milking. And Mrs Davidson, an older, rounder, ruddier version of her daughter, would ply them both with the most delicious home-made scones.

Once or twice Jenny's father, the shepherd, came in from the hill and joined them – that is, he joined in the eating and drinking, but hardly in the conversation, for he was a man of few words, and all of them pronounced in such a broad local accent that Helen had great difficulty in making him out.

Jenny told her that once Mr Morton had insisted on her father's taking a weekend off – the first in his life. With great difficulty the shepherd had been prevailed upon to go with his wife to spend the weekend with some relatives ten miles away. He had never been so far from home in his life, and was so miserable that he had insisted on going home that very same evening. Helen marvelled at Jenny's ability to be at home in the modern world, to talk about films and clothes and dances, while yet living in harmony with a father who had never left his home and hillside, not even for one whole day. Jenny, it seemed, had a genius for harmony.

Spring turned to early summer, and the place became a paradise of flowers and fresh young leaves. As she followed the track through the patches of blazing green bracken, Helen could hardly believe that here she was, at five o'clock in the morning, on her way to work, and enjoying it. In the city, five in the morning is a dismal hour. Either you're up far too early, or you're up too late, and beginning to feel jaded. But the freshness about her was so intense, the colours so glowing, that long before she had climbed over the first five-bar gate, the last traces of sleep had left her. She felt she was living in Traherne's radiant childhood world. 'The corn was orient and immortal wheat,' she murmured to herself.

And yet, and yet, she could not settle. In spite of this constant sense of paradise, she could not settle. She loved it all, admired it, felt welcomed by it, yet knew that she was alien to this world. With the quotation from Traherne still fresh in her mind, the word 'corn' found a new juxtaposition, and became 'alien corn'. Nothing and nobody here had said 'You'll never be like one of us,' and yet she knew that this was so.

She became more and more unsettled and began to feel ill again. The impending end of the war added to her restlessness. Soon it would be all over anyway, and she would have no place here. Normal life would be resumed, for better or for worse, and she would have no claim on Arcadia.

When her mother broke her leg a few weeks later Helen was forced to go home and look after her. She left her alien paradise with relief and regret. She would miss it all terribly, even though she was going back to her own life. She would miss the hills and the bracken, the people and the cows, Jenny and Mona. Especially Mona.

On the last morning, after the milking was over, she left Jenny in the dairy and slipped back into the byre to say goodbye to the cows. She started at the end near the door and gave a valedictory pat to each cow as she passed her.

Then she came to Mona. More than a pat was required here. Throwing an arm round the animal's neck she leaned against her and stood there, gently rocked by Mona's breathing. She wished Mona would turn her head and give her a parting look. But of course, the cow couldn't know this was to be the last time. And even if she did, would she care? Again Helen wondered what it was that made her feel this special link with Mona.

She was toying with the idea of having known her in a previous incarnation when Jenny appeared at the door.

'That you saying goodbye to your favourite cow?' she asked, smiling.

'Yes, I suppose she *is* my favourite. I don't quite know what it is we have in common, but there must be something.'

'Of course there is,' said Jenny. 'You're both different from the herd, that's what it is. A grey cow's a rather unusual animal in this part of the country. And you're pretty different yourself, not like the rest of us plain folks.' She said this without a shadow of blame or criticism – just a statement of fact, which Helen accepted almost with relief. Yes, that was it. She was what she was. Not necessarily better or worse. Just different.

'They'll miss you, you know,' said Jenny, nodding at the cows.

'Will they notice?'

'Oh, yes. They'll notice. They'll be a bit unsettled at the milking for a day or two. They'll miss you all right. We all will,' she added, identifying herself with the cows. 'Especially Mona.'

14

The Song of the Rising Sap

As soon as he saw the bend in the river far below he knew this would be a good place to hear the voices. He stopped and got out of the car, and stood for a long time leaning against the stone dike, looking down. There was only one field between him and the stream, and the ground fell steeply, so he had a good view of the flat little valley with the water twisting its way along. Vague memories of school geography suggested to him that this was a U-shaped valley – flat bottom, steep sides, with a river meandering between.

He felt he wanted to classify this place in his mind, before handing himself over to it.

What had made it clear to him that this was the place he was looking for was the sight of the oxbow loop in the river. He had seen these things on maps, places where the bend of the river is so pronounced that it almost comes back to its starting point. This one had left a round peninsula in the water, an almost-island. From where he stood he guessed it must be fifteen to twenty feet in diameter. Quite big enough for him to pitch his tent on.

And the really most enchanting thing about all this was the fresh green of the grass on the little circle of land. Of course, he thought, it has to be. Permanently surrounded by water. Perfect conditions for the grass to grow in. And for the voices, too.

He stood there for a while, savouring the moment. The

moment when you've found what you're looking for. Then he started getting his gear out of the car. It would have been more prudent, no doubt, to make sure first that the ground was suitable for camping. Still, he decided he would risk it. He would make his act of faith. The voices, he felt sure, would appreciate that.

When he got to the water's edge and crossed the narrow tongue of land that joined the semi-island to the mainland he saw that he had made the right decision. The ground on the magic circle was firm, smooth and dry. The grass was so lush and so even that it seemed almost ungrateful to put down a groundsheet.

Once the tent was up and everything in position, he sat down on the grass near the water's edge. It was still early evening, so he knew he had plenty of time to wander along the river bank. But he reminded himself that he hadn't come here to explore. He had come to listen to the voices. And the voices valued stillness. The exploration could wait till tomorrow.

He could hear voices already, of course. The voice of the stream, the cries of birds, the rustling of the fresh green leaves on the big ash tree just a little way up the hill, the occasional plop as a fish rose to the surface for a fly and then dived down again. Wonderful noises, full of the beauty of relevance. But these were not the only voices he had come to hear. He was hoping for a more inward sound, something that would speak from the very heart of things.

He had heard the voices before now, in the quiet evening breeze, in the almost soundless beating of a bird's wings; he had heard the heartbeat of the hare standing near him, unaware of his presence, and the sound of the rising sap in the old oak tree in his garden. As he sat there he thought about the unique, unrepeatable quality of these sounds.

He would have liked to share them. But where would you

get a delicate enough instrument? And who would be the performer? And what notation could you possibly devise? He thought of Messiaen and the influence of birdsong in his music. That in itself had been quite a *tour de force*. But, after all, what Messiaen was doing was infinitely far from the special alchemy he had in mind. The composer was using a dazzlingly wide range of already existing instruments to capture or evoke sounds that were already familiar to most people. We have all heard the sound of the nightingale – or, if we haven't, we can easily hear it on tape. But who can convey the song of the rising sap?

Who, after all, can hear it? That was where the fundamental difficulty lay. The other problems were matters of technique. To find an instrument and a player and a notation were technical problems, and as such ultimately soluble. Problems of technique always are, in the long run. No vacuum exists between demand and supply. The history of technology seems to prove this.

And where did his capacity to hear these things come from? Had he evolved further than his fellow men in this respect? Or had he retained a faculty that the majority had lost? He was inclined to believe the latter, on the supposition that our mental faculties have become so acute that our other perceptions may have been blunted in the process. He felt sure that long ago we shared with the animals, the birds and the fish and the insects, an ability to perceive things we cannot even begin to imagine.

He stretched out on the grass, trying to quieten his mind by relaxing his body. He hadn't come here to speculate. He had come to listen. He rolled over on to his side and rested his head on his arm. And gradually he began to hear. And the voices this time were coming from beneath him. Little by little he began to distinguish the sounds of what was going on in the earth.

131

At first he suspected that what he heard was no more than his own heartbeat, the circulation of his own blood. But gradually he began to distinguish different rates of vibration. Beneath and beyond the surge of his own blood there was something else – a subtler rhythm, more widespread. After a while he began to realize that the subtlety of this sound was composed of an infinite number of tiny rhythms, similar, but each with its own variations.

Eventually they identified themselves. He was listening to the vibrations of the growing grass. It was a hybrid sound, for the voice of the blades was different from that of the roots – higher, sweeter. And every blade, and every root, sang its own version of the melody. He thought of Thomas Tallis and the forty parts of his *Spem in alium*, and wondered at the infinitely greater complication of this motet.

There were other voices too. He couldn't distinguish them just yet. Deeper, darker voices. Perhaps he would be able to identify them later. Meanwhile he was content to lie still and listen to the grass. Every so often the rhythm would be disturbed by a different set of vibrations – smooth, almost oily, powerful. He suspected that a worm was burrowing its way through his particular patch of grass. Then the new vibrations would fade into the distance and the voice of the grass would recover its normal, ubiquitous whisper.

And then, over to the right, near one of the tent pegs, there seemed to be something pretty strenuous going on. A series of rhythmical vibrations, growing steadily in intensity till they reached a climax. Then they came to a halt in a sort of heavy, groaning sigh which was followed by a few seconds of silence. And then it all started again. Something big growing there, it seemed. An acorn, perhaps, struggling with its environment, perhaps even just a particularly determined beech nut. He would have to come back later in the season and see whether anything had come to the surface.

As evening began to fall he stood up and had a good stretch, stiff with lying so long in the same position. And he was beginning to feel hungry. He ate his meal sitting at the door of his tent, like a patriarch, completely surrounded by the little plot of land that he had decided to consider his own for the night. After that he thought a little exercise before turning in would be a good idea. But he was reluctant to leave his magic circle of land. He stood for a while with one foot on the isthmus, but couldn't make up his mind to step back on to the mainland. No, he decided, he would stay where he was. He would just walk round and round the peninsula. So he walked round its edges, circling the tent, for quite a few minutes, thinking of the power of the circle.

By walking round in this way he was affirming the supremacy of the circle as pattern and as symbol. Older and more potent and more basic than the cross or the arrow or any other icon he could think of. He was happy to be paying homage to the circle in this way. It seemed a fitting thing to do in such a place. It would help to keep him in tune with the voices.

He walked till it was almost dark. Then he went into the tent and lay down, prepared to start listening again. He didn't know how long it would be till the voices lulled him to sleep. But it didn't matter. He would just listen as long as possible and accept what sleep the voices accorded him.

It wasn't long before he was able to hear the voice of the grass once again. And the acorn or beech nut, or whatever it was, that was still pushing away for all its worth.

After a while he decided it was time to try and tune his ear to the deeper, darker sounds he had half heard earlier on. This proved more difficult than he had expected. He was aware of a sort of distant rumble, but that was as far as he could get for a long time. Above it, and dominating it, was the sound of the grass. Bit by bit, however, the darker sound began to acquire more definition. At first it sounded as an intermittent, deep groan. Gradually he began to distinguish a regular, warlike rhythm to these sounds. And as he listened it seemed to him that the voice of the grass was beginning to waver slightly. And both tendencies increased, till the grass seemed to be keening in a frightened lament, and the subterranean growls grew stronger and more thunderous all the time.

The combination of these conflicting sounds was deeply disturbing. He lay listening in growing disquiet, feeling as if he were witnessing some cosmic struggle between the forces of good and evil. He tried to sleep, but Armageddon was raging beneath him, and sleep refused to come. He sat up and covered his ears with his hands, but that was no good, he could still feel the vibrations.

After a while he lay down again, deeply distressed, and must have fallen asleep at last, for he woke up with a cry of terror. What he was afraid of he couldn't possibly define, but the terror was immense, and he couldn't tell whether it simply came from his awareness of the battle going on in the ground below him, or whether some other even more terrifying element had appeared in his dream.

Whatever it was, he could bear it no longer. He struggled to his feet and rushed out of the tent. The only thing to do was to climb back up to the road and spend the rest of the night in the car.

Outside the tent it was very dark. No moon, no stars, not a hint of dawn. Cautiously he approached the part where he expected to find the narrow tongue that would lead him to the field. It took him quite a while to find it in the dark, and he almost gave way to panic at one point, imagining that the link with the mainland had been swept away, and that he was now stuck on the little island, marooned.

When at last he found his way back to the field he

scrambled up the steep side, stumbling, actually falling, picking himself up, struggling on again. At last he came to the dike, and on the other side found the road and the parked car.

He spent the rest of the night huddled up in the back of the car, wishing he had had the foresight to bring his sleeping bag with him. But he suspected it would take more than a sleeping bag to stop the shaking and shivering that possessed him.

He waited till it was broad daylight before even venturing to look down at the green circle with his tent pitched on it. The whole scene was as enchanting and innocent looking as it had been the previous afternoon, with an added radiance from the morning light.

He set off down the hill again, wondering if he would ever know what it was that had so upset him. What sort of a struggle was going on in the depths of that little peninsula?

Standing by the side of the stream he gazed thoughtfully at its rocky bed. It struck him that under the topsoil on the green circle there must be some particularly hard rock, to have withstood the constant attack of the river, forcing the water to take a circuitous route round it. Had there perhaps been some minor earth tremor last night that had set the roots of the grass at odds with the bed on which they rested? And then it occurred to him that, as his awareness descended deeper and deeper, it had tapped the level at which the root is joined in battle with the sheer rock. What he had experienced had perhaps been the eternal struggle of organic against inorganic matter.

He collected his things, crossed over to the field, laid everything down and turned to the circle once again. He didn't want to leave it till he felt he was no longer at odds with it. He would walk round it once more. And then he remembered how he had done this, repeatedly, before going to bed. And he remembered how he had been thinking of the power of the circle. Perhaps this – the actual circling, or even just his own preoccupation with the circle and its powers – perhaps this had something to do with his acutely heightened state of perception. You never know.

For a moment he hesitated. Then he moved forward and started walking, in the opposite direction from the previous night. After all, if he had cast a spell on the place with his circling, he wanted to leave it undone.

For he would come back. Yes, he would come back some time, fresh after a good night's sleep, to look for any signs of life from whatever was working so hard at getting its leaves above ground. And he fixed his eyes on the spot, to be sure to know where to look.

And he might even have the courage to listen to the voices again. By then he would have got used to the idea of what was probably going on. He would have come to accept the everlasting struggle between root and rock. And, secure in his awareness of the eternal balance, he would be able to witness the battle again, this time with equanimity.

Yes, he would come back and listen to the voices once again. And who knows what others might be added? He set off up the hill, back to the car, wondering at what frequency fluid magma vibrates.

15

The Wall

The soldiers came and demolished the village. It took them only a few minutes. They drove a tank through the single row of huts that constituted the one and only street. The huts crumbled like matchboxes, and by the time the tank had reached the end of the row there was nothing left but a dense cloud of dust hanging over a long heap of rubble. The soldiers drove on, laughing, to demolish the next village. After the silence had been complete for some time the people began to creep back cautiously from the forest where they had hidden as soon as the scout arrived with the news that the soldiers were on their way. By now the dust had settled and the villagers were able to see the long line of rubble that had been their homes. One of the middle huts had somehow managed to retain one standing wall – the front one, with its door and tiny window, almost as if nothing had happened. Only the difference was that the rectangles of door and window, instead of showing up dark against the white wall, were now bright with the early morning sunlight streaming through them, making the wall look darker in comparison. This reversal of the natural order made it clear at once that the rest of Leocadia's house had not been spared. The façade stood there like a parody of a triumphal arch, as the ironic centrepiece of a long line of ruins.

As the people came out of the forest and saw what had become of their village they began to wail. First one voice, then another, rose in a loud and piercing lament. The people advanced, and the wailing grew in volume and intricacy, into a weird and complex fugue of desolation and despair. Each family was drawn to their own little plot of rubble to lament their private loss. Gradually, still wailing, they gathered in front of the one standing wall. Leocadia stood among them, silent, facing her own open door. It was as if they all expected some sort of sign or command from this one remaining symbol of their community. Gradually the wailing began to die down, then stopped abruptly. The unrehearsed ceremony of lamentation was over, and the people dispersed. Now each went to his own plot to see what could be rescued. Leocadia was left standing alone, still silent. Soon scraps of conversation could be heard from the various groups, and families began drifting away, carrying as much as they could in the way of food and belongings. No farewells were said; it was taken for granted that they were all heading for the same place – over the hills, to the more peaceful regions in the hinterland.

'Leocadia, you are alone, you must come with us. We must all help each other.'

'No, María, I'll stay here.' Leocadia looked at her next-door neighbour of more than forty years and reflected that this might be the last time they ever saw each other.

'But Leo, it's not safe here. They will come back. And if they don't, others will. You have no one to protect you. Not even a house to live in.'

'I have a wall. I still have my front door. That's more than you have,' Leocadia smiled gently.

'And what use is a door, in God's name? What use is a wall without a house? It won't even keep the rain off you.'

'It never rains. You know it never rains now.'

'Well, it won't even keep the sun off you.'

'Yes, it will. All morning its shade will keep me cool

here, in the street, and all afternoon I can take shelter on the other side, where my house used to be. Only at midday . . . '

'At midday you will be roasted like a peanut in a burning fiery furnace.'

'Only for a few hours. We can all stand a few hours of discomfort.'

María's husband now appeared. 'You're coming with us, Leocadia. You can't travel alone.'

'No, Pedro, I must wait for my son.'

'He may not come, Leocadia.'

She bowed her head in acknowledgement.

'He has been gone many months.'

Again she bowed her head. 'But I must wait.'

Pedro and María exchanged glances, unconvinced. Then María tried again. 'But you cannot stay here without a house. And the soldiers may come again.'

'They would kill you,' put in Pedro.

Leocadia smiled deprecatingly. 'I am very old,' she said.

'But you are strong and active. You can easily keep up with the rest of us.'

Leocadia smiled again, almost apologetically. 'It's not that. How can I explain? When you are young you say, "I must have this thing to be happy, I must have this other thing to be safe." But when you are old, truly, blessedly old like me, then things don't matter so much. This thing or that thing, you take from them what you wish. So I shall wait here. If my son comes, that is good. And if the soldiers come, that is good too.'

'And if no one comes?'

'Perhaps that would be best of all.'

By now all the other families had gone. María and Pedro bade a ceremonious farewell to their neighbour and set off, carrying as much as they could. After they had gone a few yards María turned and called back, 'Leo, you will find half a sack of meal in the corner by the window. We've taken all we can carry. Take it, with our blessing.'

Leocadia bowed her head and spread out her hands in a gesture of acceptance. She watched her friends till they had disappeared over the crest of the hill, then she turned round to face the front of her house, and stood there, very still.

She was doing penance. I shouldn't have left the village, she thought, I shouldn't have left it unprotected. When the news of the advance of the soldiers had come she had decided to stay. She didn't know how a solitary old woman could withstand the soldiers and their tanks. But she had a strong conviction that this was what she ought to do. As the oldest member of the community she would intercede for the village. But she had let herself be flustered and frightened by the fear of the others, scooped up by their panic in the uneasy half-light of dawn.

Now she stood in front of the devastation that by her own weakness she had not managed to prevent, trying to recover her centre. She had lost what might be her last chance of doing anything for another human being. She had bungled it. Now she had to recover her harmony with the physical world, with this little part of the earth's surface that she knew and belonged to.

After a while of emptiness she began to lay her plans, to settle how she was to live this next, and perhaps last, phase of her life.

She would do as she had said to María, get as much shade as she could from her one remaining wall. She wandered about among the ruins till she found a little rush-bottomed chair a few houses away. Anselmo's chair, she thought. He will not need it. He will not grudge me it. She thought of how often she had sat on it outside Anselmo's front door, and dusted it carefully with her apron. Then she carried it

140

back to her own house. At that precise moment she had no need for it, as the sun was so high that neither side of the wall afforded much shadow. However, she set to, and, having cleared a space near the door, she placed the chair in it, so that it would be ready for her when the sun once again agreed to share its power with the shadows. Then she moved to the corner of the hut where her bed had been – still was, in fact, though buried under a large portion of roof. Carefully and without hurrying she cleared the debris off the bed, took the bedding out through the front door, and, obeying an urge to keep to the familiar rituals, shook it out thoroughly. After that she brought it back in again and carefully remade the bed on top of the debris she had cleared off it.

If I can't sleep under my own roof, she thought with a smile, at least I shall sleep on top of it.

Her next move was to hunt about a bit till she found a few utensils to eat out of – a tin plate, a spoon, a cup. She decided not to bother making a fire. She would eat the meal soaked in water, that would do well enough. The prospect of living at this very basic level filled her with a certain satisfaction. It was a new beginning, with all the excitement and stimulation that this brings, and at the same time a going back to a more primitive stage. It wasn't that she didn't appreciate the good things of this earth – she had thoroughly enjoyed the few and simple luxuries that had come her way. But she had always tried to limit her needs and her desires, not through asceticism or a desire to punish herself, but out of an unshakeable conviction that there lay contentment.

The more you have, the more you want, had been her motto.

Having found a mound of rubble near the door, where her table used to stand, she placed a flat piece of wood on it. Now she had a table again. Before putting her small assortment of implements on it she reflected that it would be better with a cloth. Finding one of the curtains relatively undamaged she gave it a good shake and installed it as her tablecloth. Now all she needed was to see to the water and the corn supplies, and she would be ready to start her new regime.

The well, which was a few yards beyond one of the end houses, was undamaged. Even the bucket and rope were in perfect order. She drew water and carried it slowly to the new version of her home. Now that there was no-one else in the village she could just leave the bucket there, inside her front door – or outside, in the morning, to take advantage of the only source of shade. She would have transferred María's half sack of corn to her own house, but delicacy forbade her to do this. It belonged to María and Pedro, and in their house it must stay, even though they had given it to her. But she would gladly help herself to a portion, morning and evening, always remembering to give thanks in her heart to the givers.

After the meal, sitting in the shade behind her wall, she looked out of her doorway on to the familiar sandy surface of the road. Apart from a few pieces of debris left lying about, all she saw looked perfectly normal, just as for the past forty years. An ant hill near her door had been trampled on, and the ants were busily repairing the damage. They're doing just what I've been doing, she thought, only better. But then, they have a purpose to fulfil together. Her purpose was now a solitary one. She sat for a long time watching the ants with great concentration, reflecting that never before in her life – not since early childhood, at any rate – had she been able to enjoy unlimited time to sit and do nothing. It was pleasant, she thought, a good way of growing. Life had cast her in the role of one of the Marthas of this world; but the Mary inside her, developing slowly and fitfully, could now come into her own. She had always been a doer and a helper and a contriver, coping with gusto in the face of poverty and difficulties. Now for the first time there was nothing to do. No one needed her help – not the help of her hands, anyway.

For days she sat there, reliving the incidents of her life one after another. How, she wondered, could people talk of being lonely, with this unending procession going on inside? All her friends were there, her children, her husband, neighbours, strangers, all the people she had ever known, the living and the dead. Even people she had merely heard about, they were all there, familiar from the words of her companions. Now that there were no things to be done, no people to interrupt her, she held discourse with a refreshing company. Many, if not most of them, were dead, but that made no difference.

Over the years, she had noticed, she grieved less over each succeeding death. It was as if the boundary between life and death became blurred as the years rolled on. She thought of the bitter grieving of her youth over the death of her first child. She recalled the loss she had felt when her husband had died all those years ago; and now it all seemed a mistake, an unnecessary agony. And she thought of her one remaining son, long overdue from his journey. But she thought of him without fear, even without apprehension. The wall that separated the living from the dead had become increasingly fragile. Her son might be on this side of it, he might be on the other. Either way, it didn't much matter. It was all a question of time.

This blurring of the frontiers between the living and the dead was an affective thing. It was not in any sense a case of mental confusion. She knew very well who was living and who was dead. It was just that she felt as close to the one as to the other. She had come to feel that death was a relatively unimportant stage in the development of all living creatures.

Every night she slept very peacefully in her bed under the stars, almost without dreams. When she got up she always stood for a while outside her door, facing east, as she had that first day when the huts were knocked down. But now she stood calmly, without the self-reproach of that first day. She had failed then, but now her failure was over, now she had another part to play in this arid strip of world that was still her home. She was trying to become perfectly, totally at one with this wonderful patch of dusty soil. She wanted to belong to it as completely as the ants moving lightly over its surface. She wanted to become the place itself, just as the dry and dusty road was the place and the dark green forest beyond was also the place. She wanted to assume the consciousness of this piece of soil that she had known and served all her life.

On the seventh morning she woke up more refreshed than ever. She was sure she had had no dreams, just a long consciousness of sleep and rest. And with it an awareness that someone was travelling through the forest, coming towards her. She got up and stood as usual in front of her wall, facing east, with her back to the forest. She had no idea how near or how far the traveller was, and felt no temptation to turn and look. Her seven solitary days had washed away all curiosity or impatience. She imagined the swish of the machete clearing a path through the forest. She stood there waiting for the actual sound to come to her. Perhaps the traveller was her son. Or perhaps a stranger. Or perhaps the hand that wielded the blade was carrying not a machete, but a scythe.

16

Hard Folk

They say I'm a hard man. I hope they're right. It's my only chance.

There's no other choice. You're either hard or soft. Hard like me, like all those other buggers out there, or soft, like Annie here. Soft and sullen. Too weak to get her way, too stubborn to stop wanting it. Wanting without ever really trying. And that's what makes her sullen. She has to accept my way of things, but she won't, not inside her.

But at least she leaves me in peace. Black looks, and whimpers and sighs, a man can live well enough with them. Just ignore it all, and you've wiped her out completely. She's still there, getting on with the job of being a working farmer's wife, which is all I wanted her for. But not there as a force to be reckoned with.

And she can't complain, can't say I deceived her. Not one word of love or any of that nonsense passed my lips.

'Annie,' I said, 'you're a good worker. I've seen you at the milking, and out shawing turnips with the frost thick on the shaws, and your hands blue with cold, and a snell wind blowing from the east; and you working, working.'

That's all the soft words I gave her. And I told her I was looking for a wife. 'I'm thinking you might suit me,' I said.

'Oh, Robert!' she said, and gave me a melting look. I think she was hoping for fine words. But she got none. I wasn't going to deceive her. I'm a hard man, but honest. She can't complain.

'So that's it settled,' I said.

And that was it settled.

She knew why I'd picked on her, of course. Not just the way she could work. Her father was dying of TB, we all knew that. Her only brother had already died of it, and her mother had died in childbed years earlier. Just Annie and the old man left, and the farm, of course.

Mind you, it was a risk. I knew I was taking a risk. She might have died of TB too, she might have passed it on to me. But it was the only way a man in my position could get any land of his own. If I hadn't taken that chance I'd still be working as a hind, working to another man, with no hope of ever being master. Just a common byreman, like poor Geordie here. He knows he's of less value than any of the cows he milks. Working from dawn to dusk, sleeping in the loft above the scullery, that's his life. But it's not so bad for the likes of him. You can accept these things if you're a bit wanting.

But me, I'm different. I've got my wits about me, and can see what's what. Geordie's thankful to have a place to live in, a table to eat at, and someone to tell him what to do next. But I could never live like that. I have to be my own master. Yes, *master*.

And that's the way things were for a long time, till that little bitch from the city came and spoiled it all.

She came with her long slim fingers and her posh accent and her city ignorance. Oh, yes. She'd just done a year at university studying agriculture, if you please. That's why she came to us, to spend the summer working on a farm. Supposed to be so as to get in some practical. That's what they call it, practical. But we all felt sure she'd come to tell us how it should all be done. Come to show up our ignorance.

Mind you, it would never have happened if I hadn't agreed to take a student in the first place. Cheap labour, they said. And I'm not the man to let a bargain go past him. Perhaps I should have known from the start that a student wouldn't fit in. And of course, we didn't know it was going to be a lassie. Lyndsey Morton, it said on the form. We thought it was a queer kind of way to spell the name, but then, all sorts of odd things can happen with spelling. Especially people's names. And we're not all that good at the spelling anyway, Annie and me. Even the bairns can do better. But they didn't know either.

'Someone to see you,' said Geordie, looking quite excited. I knew who it would be. This was the afternoon the student was to come. So I went into the yard and I saw this skinny creature in jeans, and a head with long hair, poking into the byre. My God, I thought, not one of those!

And then the creature turned round and spoke to me. And I saw it was a girl.

Well, I was relieved, I can tell you, to know it wasn't what I thought. I'm not having any queers on my farm. But I couldn't think who this could be.

'Can you tell me where I can find Mr Main?' Quite snooty, like.

'You're speaking to him,' I said.

'Oh, indeed? I've been sent here to help.'

'Help?'

'Yes,' she said. 'Weren't you expecting a student?'

'Aye, a student. No a lassie,' I managed to say when I'd got my wits back.

Well, there was quite a stushie, while I refused to have her and she refused to go. And Geordie standing looking at the girl, with not the slightest idea of what was going on. But he's got quite an eye for the lassies, Geordie has, and he just couldn't take his eyes off that one.

147

And that's what gave me the idea.

'We can't put you up,' I said. 'We were expecting a man. He was to share the loft with Geordie here. Don't suppose you'd fancy that, would you?'

Geordie looked as if *he* would, but the girl blushed scarlet and shook her head.

'But I've been sent here,' she insisted. 'It was all arranged. They'd even sent you my name.'

'A man's name,' I pointed out.

'Not when it's spelt like that. Everyone knows it's a girl's name when it's spelt like that.'

I think I could have forgiven her everything except that 'Everyone knows'. As good as calling me ignorant.

'Annie!' I called. 'Come and see what sort of a student they've sent us.'

Annie came and gauped. You could see she was as taken aback as I was.

'Where d'you think we're going to put this young lady, then?' I asked.

'Well, I suppose we'll just put her up in the spare room, like we meant to anyway,' bleated Annie.

I could have killed her, giving the show away like that.

'Take her up to the spare room, then.' To the girl I said, 'I expect you down here again in ten minutes to help with the milking.'

And in ten minutes she was down all right, very business-like, hair tied back, ready for work. Only she didn't even know how to handle the machines. So I set Geordie to teach her. He loved it. Fair made up for his disappointment over sharing the loft.

We'd expected a stuck-up young man, and we got a stuck-up young woman instead. That was all the difference. Not that she said very much. It was just her manner. And her accent.

148

Why could she not talk like plain folks? She lived in our house for three months, but she wasn't with us. She'd brought her own world with her, inside, and she lived in that. Never spoke to us, never spoke to the bairns. Only Geordie, she would chat away with Geordie sometimes. Perhaps it was to make us feel small, to show that even poor Geordie was more worth talking to than us.

You'd have thought the Almighty had sent that girl to humble me in every way. It wasn't just her accent and her toffee-nosed way of speaking. It was as if we didn't speak the same language. She didn't know what a graip was, or a besom or a luggie. And every time I had to explain something she would say, 'Oh, you mean a fork . . . , or a broom . . . , or a milking pail.' As if her way was the only way. As if our way, my way, was wrong.

You'd have thought she'd been sent to humble us with her appearance, too. Slim and supple and light-footed. Seeing her beside my Annie was like looking at a tender young birch beside a shapeless old whin. For Annie never had much of a figure anyway, and now . . . now she's thick and heavy and shapeless, slow and bent, yes, bent, as if she was standing at the sink all the time, peeling tatties. As if she never really had enough time to straighten up between one job and the next.

And she was a worker, too, this lass. Never once gave me the chance to scold her for idleness. She was a bit handless, you could see she'd never held a tool in her life, and ignorant, in spite of her studies and her exams, her aggro nommy and her chemistry and all the rest of it. But she'd keep at it, keep up with the rest of them, even though she looked fit to drop. Proud little bitch, that girl. Never gave me a chance to complain. And that's another thing I can't forgive her. Always in the right, she was.

149

And that meant I was always in the wrong. Well, not just me. All of us.

It was the same at meal times. Picky about her food. Didn't like stew.

'Is there nothing else?'

Couldn't drink strong tea. The first time we had haggis she asked, 'What's this?' With disapproval. Always leaving you with the feeling that she was used to something better. Putting you in the wrong, without saying a word.

And after the meal she would go straight upstairs to her room, and that's the last we'd see of her till morning.

Reading, she said.

'Studying?' Annie asked her one day.

'No. Reading for pleasure.'

Well, that put us in our place, didn't it? Knew damn well that none of us could ever get any pleasure out of reading.

Annie didn't like her any more than I did, though perhaps for different reasons. I don't think she felt humbled by her. More like threatened. As if I'd ever thought of looking twice at the girl! Not that she wasn't a bonnie enough lassie, in her way. And Annie'd never had any looks to speak of, even when she was young. And now she's just a beast of burden. That's why she felt threatened. But she never said anything. Never sticks up for herself, never feels she has any rights to stick up for. Soft.

Well, the lassie wasn't soft.

She was hard, like me. And cold into the bargain. Just didn't care how much she hurt us. She had her standards and she wasn't going to lower them to come down to our level. Too far above us even to complain. So she did as she was told, she never argued, but we knew it was because she was proud, not humble.

And that's how it went on for the full three months. Her, hard and proud and silent, never telling us we were doing it all wrong, but knowing it deep inside, and letting us see that she knew it. And me, hard and silent and humbled, raging inside. Wanting to take her by the shoulders and shake her till I'd smashed all the pride inside her, leaving her empty, empty enough to take in some of the life about her. Our life.

She'll never know the harm she did me, that girl. Till she came I was a proud man, satisfied with what I'd achieved in this life. I had my farm, my wife and children, my position with the neighbours. People respected me, feared me a little. And I could see why. And that was the way I wanted it to be. I was a hard man, and I wanted them to know it.

And then this little bitch comes along and, without saying a word, makes it clear that I am nothing and nobody.

I thought it would be all right after she'd gone, but it's made no difference. She might as well be back. She *is* back, here, deep inside me, scornful, indifferent, hard. And everything I do and everything I have, it's all wrong now, not good enough. I'm still master, but master of what?

I look at my fields and I say, three hundred acres, what's the use of three hundred acres? That's not a farm, more like a smallholding. And I look at my herd, and the cows all seem old and scrawny. And the house! We gave her the guest's bedroom, with the lace coverlet on the bed, but she said nothing, nothing.

And now she's gone. Done all the damage she could, and left us. I suppose Annie and Geordie and the bairns have forgotten all about her by now. But me, I can't forget that easy. Till she came along I was hard and proud and full of myself.

And now I'm hard and hollow.

151

17

Under the Stairs

Flu. Please postpone visit. Pearl.

Mrs Holt held the telegram between forefinger and thumb and eyed it critically.

Good, was her verdict. I didn't think she had that much sense. More than I've had on this occasion. Yes, a very good telegram. Concise, but not peremptory. And she's been realistic enough not to put 'Love, Pearl'.

Well, that simplifies matters nicely, she thought. She was quite convinced that Pearl was not in fact suffering from flu, so felt she need not bother to expend any sympathy on her. And it's always a bit of a strain, feeling sympathy for someone you don't like, so it was a relief not to have to try. Better still was the sense of liberation the telegram had brought her.

Ever since the day some weeks ago when she had written to her sister suggesting a visit, she had felt convinced she was making a big mistake. At first she had taken refuge in the thought that Pearl would probably offer some excuse for not having her. But from the moment Pearl's letter arrived without the hoped-for refusal, Mrs Holt had felt increasingly apprehensive about the approaching ordeal. How on earth could she stand a fortnight with Pearl? They had never been able to spend ten minutes in each other's company without quarrelling.

And to think that this fortnight was to be spent in Pearl's house, which would indubitably give Pearl the upper hand.

A guest is, in a manner of speaking, a prisoner in the hands of her hosts, with the added restriction that good manners forbid any complaint. Among the things that her seventy-seven years had taught Ruby Holt was a certain amount of self-knowledge; enough to recognize that in her relationship with her younger sister, she, Ruby, was the one who expected to be boss. But you really can't move into a long-ignored sister's house and take over. After a gap of so many years you have to behave like a guest, and show gratitude, submission to your hostess's arrangements, and a becoming awareness of how well you have been welcomed.

The more she thought of the prospect, the more it appalled her. Spending the fortnight alone in her house in London's dockland in the middle of the blitz seemed infinitely preferable.

What on earth had made her agree to such a suggestion? The girls, of course: Fiona and Rosie, her two boarders. As soon as they had got their holiday fixed up they started worrying about how Mrs Holt would manage on her own. Mrs Holt pointed out that she had managed very well on her own for the last thirty years, from the death of her husband till the outbreak of war.

She had then decided to take in a couple of boarders, and Rosie and Fiona had appeared, fresh from the country. They had come to work in a government office, and soon struck up a friendship with each other and with their landlady, who lost no time in deciding that they were nice girls. Nice girls who knew their place and fitted into her domestic scheme of things, and always accepted whatever she said or decided.

Except, of course, in the case of an air raid. Then they could be heard galloping down the stairs as soon as the first siren sounded. In a moment they were pounding on her door, dragging her out of bed, and hurrying their victim along to the air raid shelter. Their pretext for this unceremonious treatment was Mrs Holt's arthritis, which made it difficult for her to move quickly, especially when starting from a recumbent position.

And this was really what had brought on the whole crisis. Both girls were going north to Fiona's home for a fortnight, and threatened not to go if Mrs Holt didn't promise to get someone else for the two weeks, or else go away where she would be safe from the air raids.

The first suggestion was categorically rejected. She wasn't having anyone else moving into her house, not even for two weeks. She had done all the rearranging for the installing of the girls, and that was enough. She realized she had been incredibly lucky in her two boarders; to agree to another upheaval, even if only temporary, would be tempting Providence. As for going away, she had nowhere to go.

'But you must have someone, surely? Even a distant relation?'

'I suppose there's my sister Pearl. She's distant enough.'

'Where does she live? Australia?'

'No, Surrey. Two-hour journey by train, I know. But distant in the other sense. I haven't seen her for twenty years.'

'Well then, there you are!' Rosie beamed. 'There's your opportunity for a good get-together.'

'A Family Reunion,' suggested Fiona sardonically.

'But I don't want a get-together with Pearl. We don't get on. We don't even like each other.'

'Isn't that the same thing – getting on and liking each other?' enquired Rosie.

'No, child, it isn't. You can even love someone and not get on with them.'

'Like most husbands and wives,' put in Fiona.

'Oh, Fiona, what a cynic you are! I hate you!' exclaimed Rosie.

'All right, hate me. But you must admit we get on very well, and that rather proves my point.'

'Isn't she horrid, Mrs Holt? Always right. It's unbearable.'

Mrs Holt chuckled.

'I'm a bit that way myself,' she admitted. 'I suppose that's why Pearl can't stand me.'

Later she realized that the reference to Pearl at this point had been a tactical error, for it brought the conversation back to the problem in hand. In the end she let herself be argued into writing to Pearl, because she didn't want to worry the girls, because she was grateful to them for their concern, and perhaps most of all because she had been so tired lately that she simply hadn't the energy to prolong the argument.

And now, with the arrival of the telegram, the whole bothersome business was over. The girls had left that morning, confident that she would be in Surrey in the early afternoon. And it was too late to make other arrangements, thank goodness.

With great satisfaction, and with a few pauses for rest, she proceeded to unpack the case she had packed earlier that morning. What a joy it was to put each item back into its accustomed place!

Now that the girls had been here for so long, she had got used to the new arrangement. But it had been a big upheaval. She could have put both of them into the guest bedroom, and it would all have been much simpler. But, remembering how she had hated sharing with Pearl, she decided each girl must have a room to herself. Just at that age, even without a war on, life is difficult enough, she remembered. The least you can ask for is a refuge, a place of your own – for the times when feelings are too high, or too low, to share.

So she had moved out of her bedroom, and taken herself and her personal belongings to the living room. She *could* have moved into the sitting room. But her Scottish upbringing rebelled at the idea of not having the sacred Room available for all special occasions, however few and far between these might be. No, the Room should remain intact, in all its icy splendour.

Casting about for a space for her bed in the already rather crowded living room, she hit upon the idea of wedging it into the hollow under the stairs, opposite the fireplace. There was just enough room for the bed. With the headboard at the high end of the little recess it really fitted in very nicely. The fact that the stairs rose only a few inches above her feet was no disadvantage, except when it came to making the bed. There you had to be careful.

The experiment led her to meditate on the amount of unused space to be found in every room. Bedrooms particularly – all that space above the foot of the bed, never used at all. It seemed such a waste.

She, by contrast, congratulated herself on her use of this space. Not an inch wasted there. Sometimes as she lay in bed and heard the girls coming back late in the evening, it amused her to think that their feet, as they crept softly up the stairs, were only inches above hers.

She felt very smug and protected in her little corner, and enjoyed looking at the dying embers in the fireplace as she lay in bed. It was ironical, she thought, that it had taken a war, with all its hardships, to introduce her to the sybaritic pleasure of going to bed in a warm room.

That evening she had to admit that she missed the girls, just a little. Usually they came down about nine o'clock to listen to the news on her wireless. Then they would all have a cup of tea and a chat. Yes, she really did miss them this evening – just a little, of course.

She smiled as she thought of their leave-taking; first Fiona, very correct and undemonstrative; then Rosie, who had flung her arms round her and told her to be good, and see and be nice to poor Pearl. After that Fiona, already on the threshold, had darted back and given her a rapid, embarrassed hug. And as she turned away for the second time there was a hint of tears in the girl's eyes. Mrs Holt thought about this again as she lay in bed that night. For some time she had suspected that there was more depth of feeling in Fiona than she was ever willing to show. As a fellow Scot she knew all about that type of emotional reticence. She lay in bed thinking about how fond of both girls she had become, and of how they had brightened her rather austere life.

She was awakened by the familiar wailing of the sirens. I don't think I'll bother, she thought, feeling rather like a child playing truant. I'm just going to lie here and let the bombs fall. Somehow it seemed the most natural thing to do. She would miss the girls, she had already missed them; but everything has its good side, and in this case it was the possibility of lying snug and comfortable in bed, instead of being dragged, cold, stiff and aching, along to the shelter. No, she repeated to herself, I'll just not bother. I'm too tired. Besides . . . this might be such a good opportunity . . .

Her thoughts drifted back to a conversation they had had one evening not long ago. The girls were reproaching her with the unwillingness to go to the shelter that she had shown the previous evening.

'You could be killed if you stayed here, you know,' remonstrated Rosie.

Mrs Holt smiled. 'I am aware of that.'

'Well, then . . . ' Rosie held out both hands in an expressive gesture.

'Well, then,' mimicked Mrs Holt, 'That's perfectly true.

But we've all got to die sooner or later. And I'm seventy-seven years old.'

Fiona gave her a searching look. 'But you're not tired of life, are you?'

'Oh, no!' Mrs Holt was quite shocked at the idea. 'Not at all.'

'Then what is it?'

'Two things, really . . . No, three, I suppose. The first you'll probably find terribly trivial. It's just a matter of effort. Even simple, ordinary things take so much more effort when you're old. Sometimes it seems disproportionate to the result. And so you ask yourself, is it really worth it? And you feel that the best and most wonderful thing that could possibly happen would be just to drift gently off into sleep, for ever. But I can't expect you people to see the force of that, with all your youth and energy.

'And the second thing is that you don't need to be tired of life to be ready for death. And I expect that's also a difficult one for you young things to understand, when you've still got all your life ahead of you. It's different when most of it's behind you. And if three-score years and ten is supposed to be our allotted span, as it says in the Bible, I've already had seven years more than I'm entitled to expect. And it would be ungrateful, and greedy, and immature, to want more. If more is given, that's fine. But it would be ridiculous, even undignified, not to be prepared to let go when the time comes.'

'I can see that,' said Fiona, 'but it's not the same as refusing to take reasonable precautions to stay alive – such as going to a shelter in a raid.'

'It's almost a sort of suicide,' Rosie put in, in an awed voice.

'You could call it suicide by default,' added Fiona.

'And that brings me to my third point.' Mrs Holt took so long to continue that Rosie prompted her:

'Well, what is it?'

'Captain Oates.'

'Captain who?'

'Oates.'

'I know,' broke in Fiona. 'The man on the Antarctic expedition that walked out into the blizzard, to leave his share of food for the others.'

Rosie was shaking her head. 'I still don't understand.'

'There's quite a blizzard blowing out there these days,' said Mrs Holt. 'They call it war. We're short of supplies, and they'll probably get much shorter. Perhaps they ought to be used for the people who are young and strong enough to contribute . . . more than I can.'

'Nonsense!' exclaimed Rosie. 'Where would we be, Fiona and I, without you to look after us? And what would happen to the war effort without us?'

'I shudder to think,' laughed Mrs Holt, and the discussion ended there.

But the subject was one on which she had thought a great deal. And now, lying in bed, nursing her project, with the sirens wailing outside, she was glad she had spoken of this to the girls. If it should happen, if this was the end, the girls would at least have some sort of idea of how she felt about it.

Of all the three reasons that she had given, the one that weighed most heavily on her was the first. She was often so tired that any effort at all seemed too much. Sometimes she wondered whether this meant that her heart was giving out. Whatever the reason for her exhaustion, the prospect of lying quietly in bed instead of dragging herself out to the shelter was irresistibly appealing.

She lay listening to the confused sounds from the blackness outside. Planes and more planes – she never could tell which were ours and which theirs. Then the bombs began to fall – distant at first, then suddenly closer. So close that she felt sure her street must have been struck. Closer still . . . then a deafening crash, and the long diminuendo of falling rubble. She was almost choked by dust, and had to breathe through the bedclothes for several minutes.

When the dust had settled and she opened her eyes again, she could no longer see the embers of the fire in front of her across the room. She put out a hand and came up against a wall of rubble just a few inches from her bed. Some pieces of plaster had landed on the bed, but nothing heavy.

Apparently the upstairs floor had fallen in, perhaps the roof as well. The stairs had held firm, and this had saved her. In a way she felt it was a pity. It would have been such a quick, easy death.

Oh, well, she thought, we'll just have to make the best of things as they are. At any rate, there was a good chance that nobody would come and look for her. All the neighbours knew she was going to her sister's, and that the girls were away. After the arrival of the telegram she had gone round to Mrs Thomson's next door to tell her of her wonderful respite. But Mrs Thomson had been out, and she had forgotten to go back. So that was all right. With a bit of luck no-one would come near her for days. And by that time it might be all right. They would find her dead in bed and assume she had been killed by falling masonry; or they might think she had died of fright.

She chuckled with satisfaction over this thought.

One thing worried her a little. She had no idea how long it might take her to die, if she lay there without food or drink. She knew you could survive a long time without food; but some form of liquid was necessary. Without that it would be quicker, but would it be quick enough? What if they found her and sent her off to hospital, and carefully nursed her back to life? What a waste of a good opportunity that would be. She'd simply have to start all over again.

Later, after all the planes had flown off and the all-clear had gone, she heard voices outside. She lay very still, anxious to make the most of her chance, afraid that some busybody might come and rescue her.

The voices grew nearer, and soon she was able to make out some of the words. Then Mrs Thomson's voice, clear and definite:

'No, she wasn't in the shelter. She's gone away to her sister's in the country. And the two girls are off to Scotland, so it's all right. There's no need to waste any time on this house right now.'

The statement must have carried conviction, for the voices began to fade. Soon blessed silence reigned again. What a pity her old neighbour would never know what a service she had done her by sending the men away!

Now that the immediate danger of being found was over, now that she had declined to take the opportunity of rescue, in favour of the larger opportunity that the situation offered, Mrs Holt felt perfectly satisfied.

How good to think she'd never be called upon to make any effort ever again. How good it was, just to lie still, in silence and darkness.

Mrs Holt smiled, gave a contented sigh, and drifted off into sleep.

Some days later the following news item appeared in the local press:

After the bombing of Norton Street last Wednesday the body of Mrs Ruby Holt, (77), resident at number 21, was found lying in bed, in the middle of her shattered home. There was no evidence that Mrs Holt had been injured by falling masonry, and it is assumed that she died in her sleep. From the peaceful and relaxed appearance of the deceased it is clear that death must have occurred before the beginning of the air raid.

18

Riders

I saw them riding through the glen that day, the men hungry for death. Not their own death, no, not that, though no man could tell how the encounter would go. But each man knew that some must kill and some must die, and each man hoped that he would be the killer, not the slain. And so each man rode past with death in his heart. And hate, of course, and hate to justify it.

And I turned away, sick with the sorrow of it, and I shut myself up in the cottage, and would not look out. But I heard them passing still, I heard the hooves of their horses as they clattered through the glen to keep their appointment with death.

I will not think of Jamie, I told myself. I will not look to see if he goes with them. He is my light and my love and my very life's blood. I will not look.

Why should I stand and wave him on, and give him courage to go forth and kill another? And give him courage to be killed? I will not look.

I will not smile and wish him well. There's no well-wishing in my heart for those who play death's game.

When Kirstie came her first words were, 'Is Jamie with them?'

'How can I tell?'

'Did you not look to see?'

'I did not look.'

'Oh, Ailie, lass, and would you let him go without a word

to cheer him on? Without a parting kiss?'

'I have no words for murderers.'

'They are not murderers!' she cried. 'Brave men, they are, fighting for the cause. Our cause. How can you call them murderers?'

'They go to kill.'

'Only the enemy. Would you have him stay behind, blackened with shame? Is he to have no glory?'

I shook my head. The stone lay on my heart so heavy that I could find no words.

She sighed and left me.

Men were still riding past. Just a few stragglers now.

I looked. I stood and looked against my will. And I saw Jamie riding past, looking to see if I was there. And all my anger turned to longing and my despair held its breath. And I was going to wave and I was going to call.

'Jamie! Jamie!'

I heard the words and saw her, Kirstie, running to him. And she held up her arms, and he leaned down and kissed her full on the mouth. Then she sank down on to the grass, and I could hear her sobs. And he rode on, following the call of death. To come back blackened with another's blood, in guilt and glory.

And it's Kirstie who will welcome him, if he comes back, for she can see only the glory.

But it's the guilt I'll see, and how am I to greet the tainted hero, the man of death?

And if he never should come back at all, how can I go on living?

Riders.

19

Travelling Light

Esteban knew from the start that the shoes wouldn't fit. You could tell at a glance.

'You're sure they're not too small?' The woman looked doubtfully at the man's large, misshapen espadrilles.

'They're perfect!' he maintained stoutly.

'Perhaps you'd better try them on. There's no point in taking them if they don't fit. I mean, I could give them to someone else.'

To prove his point Esteban sat down on the doorstep, carefully undid the tapes of his rope-soled sandals, and squeezed his way painfully into the shoes. The whole process took a long time. Having no right hand slows you down badly.

The woman didn't seem to mind waiting. She stood in the street outside her front door, her hands folded across her stomach, under her apron, watching the man.

At last he stood up. He didn't dare try to walk.

'See?' he said triumphantly. 'A very neat fit.'

'Well, if you're sure, you might as well have them.' She still sounded doubtful.

He sat down to take off the shoes and put on his espadrilles. Practice had taught him how to get the long tapes round his ankles and fastened at the front. But with only one hand and the stump of his right arm to work with, it took him even longer than getting the things off. Then he untied the corners of the checked cloth in which he carried his possessions, added the shoes to his modest collection of bits and pieces, and tied the bundle up again. After that he stood up, hooked his stick under the knot, and swung the bundle on to his shoulder.

The woman had stood watching all the time, as if lost in a timeless dream, from which the man's movement seemed to waken her. She sighed and turned towards the door.

'I'd better get back in,' she said, 'there's so much work to do.'

Slowly, almost regretfully, she drew her hands out from under her apron. Then, inside the doorway, she turned and spoke the words that were evidently on her mind.

'I don't know how you manage it,' she said. 'I mean, with only one hand.'

'Practice,' he replied. 'Practice and patience. And time. I've plenty of time.'

The woman sighed again. 'Well, I'd better get on. See you next time.'

'God willing.'

As he set off he couldn't help feeling just a bit mean about those shoes. After all, he would never be able to wear them. But he could sell them, or exchange them for something else – a new pair of trousers, for instance. His old ones had given up the ghost last week, and now he had to wear his good ones all the time. A man feels vulnerable without another pair of trousers to change into.

Suppose a dog tore the seat out of this pair?

Or what if he fell asleep with a lighted cigarette in his hand and set fire to them?

Life is so full of unexpected dangers, reflected Esteban. Personally, he had long ago given up his desire for possessions. Unlike that woman, for instance. She had her house, her furniture, her patio to hang out the washing. But it all meant work. And all that sighing! No, he didn't want to be burdened with too many things. But a second pair of trousers, that surely wasn't an unreasonable thing for a man to desire!

He was heading for the hills, following his usual itinerary. More than thirty years ago, at the end of the Civil War, when he had realized that begging would have to be his life's work, he had decided to do the thing properly and in an orderly manner. And so he had worked out his circuit, taking in the more profitable villages and the more generous farms. The regularity of the routine gave him a sense of stability, of belonging, even if in a somewhat peripheral way.

The whole circuit took up three months. In that way he was able to see each of his pastures once in every season.

This was his late summer round, and the accumulated heat of months of unbroken sunshine seemed to hang in the air. Even though it was only mid morning he could feel the heat dancing and shimmering about him. He would be glad to get to his first *masia*. Enriqueta, the farmer's wife, would give him something to eat, and cool, clear water to drink. She was hardly what you would call generous, but he knew he could always count on getting something from her. She would grumble and complain about how hard times were, then give him a slice of bread with tomato rubbed on it. It was better with a trickle of olive oil on top, but her generosity didn't always rise to such abundance.

When he got to the farm he was surprised to see no signs of Enriqueta. She was usually to be found sitting on a chair inside the big arched doorway, sewing or preparing vegetables for the next meal. He looked into the big, cool entrance hall, and saw no one.

'*Ave Maria!*' he called out. A voice answered from the back of the house, and in a moment the daughter-in-law appeared.

'Oh, it's you,' she said. 'Come in, I'll get you something to eat.'

Gratefully he stepped inside, enjoying the coolness.

'Where's *senyora* Enriqueta?' he asked.

'Dead,' was the reply.

'You don't say! What did she die of?'

'Bad temper, if you ask me. She was always arguing with my husband about the farm – just couldn't accept the fact that, as the eldest son, he naturally took over on his father's death. They were having an argument about one of the fields when she suddenly fell down and was dead within a couple of hours.'

'God rest her soul!' exclaimed the tramp. 'Things will be different here without her.'

'You can say that again! Here, look at that.' The woman laid a plate down on the table and motioned him to a chair. On the plate lay a thick hunk of bread with the usual tomato, and beside it a hearty slice of smoked ham.

'That's more than she ever gave you, isn't it? Here,' she said, as she placed a dish full of olives beside the plate. 'How about that? We'll see if folks can go on saying how mean they are at *Can Mateu*. As if we were beggars, that's what it was like! And I'm not having it any more. And wine,' she added, placing a glass of coarse red wine on the table. 'She never gave you wine did, she? God rest her soul,' she added hastily.

Esteban was amazed at the change in the woman. He had always known her as a silent, withdrawn figure, kept very much in the background. While he was happy to profit from her truculent generosity, he couldn't help feeling a little ill at ease in this torrent of pent-up resentment. Besides, he was sorry about Enriqueta's death. In spite of her dreary outlook on life she had been a familiar figure, after all.

'Good wine, isn't it? It's our own. What d'you think of it?'

In answer the man rolled his eyes eloquently.

'Is your *bota* empty? Here, hand it over.'

Esteban slipped the cord of his leather wine pouch over his head and handed the thing to the woman. She took it away and brought it back heavy with wine. As he was leaving she gave him another large hunk of bread and a handful of almonds.

'You'll be going to *Can Cantonet* now, won't you? Tell them. Just see and tell them things are different here. If *they* know, the whole countryside will soon know. Beggars! They won't call us beggars any more.'

It's been an odd morning, he thought, as he set off again. First the shoes – he wasn't at all sure he hadn't got them under false pretences. And now this woman, scattering largesse in order to get her own back on a dead woman. And then he thought of how much the younger woman must have endured under the iron rule of her mother-in-law. Poor thing, he thought. Poor things, both of them, both prisoners of the land they owned. And he trudged on in his freedom, thinking of how different his life would have been if the Civil War hadn't sucked him up into its vortex.

After the war was over he had found no work in his native village in poverty-stricken Andalusia, and he had set off for Valencia on foot, with no choice but to beg for his food. But before he reached the city his discouragement overcame him, and he made his way to the railway line, convinced that suicide was the only answer to his problems. He didn't quite make it, but emerged from the trial alive, with the loss of his right hand.

Work was now out of the question. But, ironically, his disability made life easier. The maimed have an advantage over the able-bodied, when it came to begging. He knew he

169

would now be able to beg enough to live on. So he drifted northwards to Catalonia, and accepted his position in the immense begging fraternity of the post-Civil War years.

Would he have been better the other way, he wondered, with a home and a wife and children – and work, of course. It sounds good, he thought. And then you look at the people who've got all this, and you wonder. That woman in the village, sighing all the time, and the daughter-in-law at *Can Mateu*, held down all those years, and still raging, even in her triumph.

The sun was beating down pitilessly. It seemed to have an extra ferocity today, a burning, stinging quality. And the air was still and heavy with all the summer's dust.

He had nearly reached the spot where he would have to leave the road and head through the vineyards to *Can Cantonet*, a couple of miles further up. Looking in that direction he saw thick white clouds hanging over the hills. If only it would rain, he thought. It would lighten the air and refresh the earth. But the clouds didn't mean a thing. They might hang over the hills for days at a time, without yielding a drop of rain, without even coming near enough to give you a little shade.

Shade, he thought, that's what I want before I start that climb. There wasn't a tree or a bush in sight, not a building, not even a wall. And then he remembered the bridge where the road crossed the dry river bed, just before reaching the path through the vineyards. That was it. He would rest there.

In a few minutes he was scrambling down the bank, holding on to the trunk of an old carob tree. Soon he was down on the sandy river bed, plunging into the dim coolness of the shade beneath the bridge. Pure heaven, he thought, as he sat down on the sandy bed and leaned against the masonry.

Life was full of good things, if you just let yourself enjoy them. This blessed coolness, for instance. And a *bota* full of red wine. And his favourite *masia* only a couple of miles away. And to think that he once wanted to kill himself!

After all those years the memory of that incident was still as vivid as ever. As he drowsily recalled it he seemed to hear once more the sound of the approaching train. At first just the slight vibration he could feel in the rail on which his head was resting. Then it resolved itself into a sound, just a far-off rumble. And then the rumble increased to a roaring which turned into a terrifying bellow. And then, just as the monster was about to devour him, his animal reflexes took over and he leapt up and flung himself clear – or almost clear. As the train roared past it hit, and shattered, his right hand.

That was all.

Suddenly now he realized that the roaring was in the present, not the past, and that instead of receding it was getting louder. Looking up, he saw a six-foot wall of reddish water rushing down the river bed. He scrambled to his feet and flung his arms round the tree trunk just as the full force of the torrent hit him. For a few moments he held on, while the water struggled to possess him. His greatest fear was that the force of the flood would be too much for the old, half rotten tree. But it held firm, and soon the water began to subside, and he was able to climb back up to the road.

He stood still, too shaken to think of anything but the fact that he was still alive.

He was soaked to the skin, and the delightful sense of coolness he had felt under the bridge had now turned to bitter cold, for the rain that had caused the flood up in the hills had now advanced and was falling heavily. He had lost his stick and his bundle with his few worldly goods in it – all swept out to sea. For a while he felt miserable and forlorn, too depressed even to continue his journey.

171

And then he noticed that his *bota* was still slung round his neck. After a comforting draught of the wine he began to feel better. Then the sun broke through, and he knew his clothes would soon be dry. He felt in his pocket and discovered he still had his knife. Good, he thought, that means I can make myself another stick.

As for his other possessions, they too had disappeared along with the checked cotton square that contained them. Not that there was anything of value, apart from the shoes. He knew he would re-accumulate all the other bits and pieces in the course of time.

He set off again, slowly climbing the terraced vineyards that led to the farm, his equanimity restored. The air felt fresh and vital again. The sun was beginning to dry his clothes.

His biggest problem would be how to replace the cotton square. Without it there was no point in acquiring any other possessions. Yes, he must get another cotton square as quickly as possible. The woman at *Can Cantonet*, perhaps?

He thought of the shoes, and looked longingly out to sea. Well, he'd felt all along that they weren't really meant for him. He'd just have to wait till someone else offered him a pair. And this time they might even fit!

20

The Message

He crossed a field with sheep in it, climbed over the style that straddled a wall high enough to keep the deer out, and found himself in open country. No more walls, fences or hedges, just open moorland. Slowly he began to follow the path that would lead him to the col. Once there he could decide whether to go right on up to the summit.

The idea of climbing to the top and then throwing himself over the cliff face was certainly very appealing. That would show them, anyway. But the trouble about suicide as a weapon of revenge is that you cannot, by definition, be there to see its effect. That being the case, was suicide worth the effort? And the sacrifice? Assuming there was anything left in his life to be sacrificed.

Looking up he saw a figure coming down the path towards him, still some way off. It was a shepherd, surrounded by a flurry of dogs herding along an affronted-looking sheep.

As they passed each other the shepherd gave the countryman's typical sideways nod and uttered the word 'Aye' on an indrawn breath.

Normally Martin would have stopped and exchanged a few words with the man. He knew this part of the country and its people, and got on well with them. But today he was too upset to do more than return the greeting with a grunt and a nod. It was enough, he knew. He had often witnessed country people greeting each other in this monosyllabic way.

Almost at once he regretted not having spoken. Some sort of human contact, even on the most casual level, might have been a comfort. The shepherd was an elderly man, with an air of repose about him. Martin felt that a few words with this stranger might have done him good. But it was too late now.

As he continued his climb it struck him that, if he carried out his intention, this might be the last person he was ever to see. And the parsimonious greeting from the shepherd might perhaps be the last word he was ever to hear. It seemed peculiarly inappropriate that it should be the affirmative 'Aye'. Everything inside him was saying 'No', loudly and desperately. The shepherd's 'Aye' belonged to a different world, a world of order and controlled emotions and acceptance. In short, a world of the bearable.

More intent on the turmoil within him than on the world about him, he strode on, following the path. He could see as far as the col, a long way ahead of him, with the mountain towering above that. The cliff face shone, hard and glittering, in the afternoon light.

After a while he stopped and looked back. The shepherd and his convoy had disappeared, hidden by the curve of the hill. Then he noticed something dark appearing in the distance below him. A dog, perhaps? Whatever it was, it soon stopped moving.

Martin lost interest and resumed his climb, which was now getting steeper. After a few hundred yards he stopped again. The cliff face seemed no nearer. He turned and looked downhill again, to convince himself that he was indeed making headway. The black thing had come a lot closer. It was now quite clearly a dog. Almost as soon as he saw it the animal stopped too. It stood there motionless, looking uphill towards Martin.

Next time he stopped and turned round the same thing happened. He could now make out that it was a black and white collie. It might have been any of the dogs he had seen with the shepherd, but he couldn't be sure. Most working dogs looked much the same to him. This one was still not near enough for him to make out any details. And anyway, he hadn't paid much attention at the time. All he had noticed was the sheep's offended manner, and the old man's tranquil face.

By now he was quite intrigued by the dog's behaviour, and paused again quite soon to look back. Again, the animal stopped almost as soon as he did and just stood there, looking at him. Once again it had gained some ground. Odd, he thought. What on earth was it up to? He began to feel a bit uncomfortable about this pursuit, convinced that the animal was following him deliberately. But why? And why did it stop every time he did? He couldn't understand it. God, he thought, things are bad enough without having a bloody hound tracking me.

He turned to look again, and the animal sat down without taking its eyes off its prey. For Martin felt quite sure now that the dog was after him. This time it was so close that he could hear its panting breath as it sat and watched him.

Ignore it, he told himself. He set off again. He was now within a few minutes' walk from the col. After that the real climb would start. He knew it was rough going, especially coming down. Only, this time he wouldn't need to bother about the coming down bit. That would be easy.

'Dead easy,' he murmured grimly.

Suddenly he heard a rushing noise beside him and the dog shot past, then came to an abrupt halt about ten yards ahead of him. It turned round at once and settled down as before, its eyes on Martin. The animal was now between him and the col. He advanced a few more yards, and the dog began to growl. Martin didn't fancy a head-on confrontation, and decided to try and outflank the beast.

He turned to the right and walked in that direction for about twenty yards. Then, very gradually, he began veering towards the col again. The dog bounded across and stationed itself some ten yards ahead of Martin, growling gently. When he moved towards it the growls became louder and more threatening, and the animal's teeth were bared. Martin saw the long white fangs, and a shiver of fear ran through him.

This is ridiculous, he told himself. If you're going to throw yourself over a cliff, what does it matter if you're savaged by a crazy sheepdog on the way? He tried to advance, but his legs refused to carry him. Suddenly he felt he was on the point of collapse. The distress inspired by the dog's inexplicable pursuit had combined with the stress and misery that had brought him here in the first place.

He looked about him and saw a large stone a few feet away. He would sit on that, he decided, and let fate take its course. He managed to stagger over to the stone and sat down, facing the dog.

The animal stood perfectly still for some time, as if considering this new move. Then it advanced slowly. Martin felt sick with apprehension. He wanted to lift his arms to protect his face, but was unable to move. The dog walked right up to him, looking at him with earnest eyes. Then it dropped its head and stood still, with its forehead pressed against Martin's knees. Martin sat motionless, filled with a mixture of relief and surprise.

After a moment the dog looked up with eager, troubled eyes, and began to whine gently, insistently. Martin felt certain it was trying to tell him something.

176

'What is it, old fellow?' he asked. The dog whined again and licked his hand. Then it swivelled round so that it stood beside him, its body leaning against Martin's thigh. He put his hand on its back, too weak and tired to stroke it. But he felt the dog's warmth under his hand and along his thigh, and with the warmth came a great sense of peace.

They sat for a long time like this, looking towards the cliff face.

Suddenly the dog's head shot up, its ears pointed and tense. A distant whistle had sounded from the direction of the valley. The dog moved a few paces away, then turned to look again at Martin with all its old earnestness.

'That's it, old chap, that's the boss calling, You'd better go.'

The dog made as if to go off, then turned back again, whining, and licked Martin's face.

Again the whistle sounded. This time the dog gave a loud yelp and set off again, bounding down the hill. Martin watched till it was out of sight. Then, utterly exhausted, he slid off the stone and stretched out on the grass.

For some time his mind grappled vainly with the puzzle of why the dog had behaved in this way. It had a message for him, he was sure of that. But what was it trying to say?

He sat up and leaned against the stone, looking down into the valley, half hoping to see the dog again. Then he turned and looked at the cliff face towering high above. Would he really have thrown himself over? Perhaps, if it hadn't been for the dog. Yes, if it hadn't been for the dog, by now he would be very near the top, with his mind still dominated by thoughts of revenge and destruction. Not only self-destruction, of course. He wanted to destroy a lot more than that with his own death. If the dog hadn't come, heading him off . . .

He stood up, gave a last look at the cliff face, and began

to walk down, following the path the dog had taken. If he hurried he might just manage to meet up with the shepherd. Not that he wanted to speak to him any longer. It was the dog he wanted to see again, to make sure it knew he had finally got the message.

21

Golden Means

'Tell you what, you can have it for ten quid.'

Thomas looked at the man in front of him and decided he wouldn't even buy a box of matches from him. Never seen a more slippery-looking customer. The large, flabby frame was not prepossessing, the clothes were shabby, almost ragged . . . And as for the face – yes, that was the least reassuring thing about the whole person. Slack, flaccid flesh, grey with dirt or ill-health, loose, thick lips, with a moustache above them to give a suggestion of decisiveness, several chins with a covering of reddish-grey stubble. And small, rat-like eyes staring at him with a disturbing intensity. Discoloured hair of the haystack variety under a greasy cap.

Ugh!

'Ten quid,' repeated the man. 'It's a bargain, I tell you.'

He gave a little shake to the bicycle he was supporting. His left hand was on the saddle, his right on the handlebars. And the little shake just about lifted the bicycle off the ground.

Hmm! Must be stronger than he looks. Or perhaps it's a very light bicycle. What I've always wanted.

'Can't afford bargains.'

The man looked at him speculatively. 'Poor student, that it?'

Thomas nodded, wondering whether he had Poor Student

written all over him. Or had the man made inquiries, perhaps?

'Then all I can say is, if you're a poor student, mate, you can't afford not to snap up a bargain like this. Here,' and he pushed the bike over towards its prospective buyer, 'have a go. That'll convince you more than anything I can say. Go on.'

If I start riding that thing, there's no telling what might happen. I've wanted a bicycle ever since I came here. And ten pounds! It's absurdly cheap. Must be stolen.

The man took both hands off the bicycle, giving it a slight push in Thomas's direction as he did so. Thomas had no option but to put his hands on the thing, to prevent it falling against him. His right hand closed on the saddle, his left on the handlebars.

Feels good, the cold chromium under one hand, the softer, warmer feel of the leather under the other.

Thomas sighed with longing.

'The thing is,' the man went on, 'I can't ride it myself. That's why – and I'm sure an observant chap like you has noticed this – that's why I'm on the wrong side of the bicycle. Doesn't really matter what side you're on, does it, if you're not going to get on it, if all you can do is push the damn thing.'

If it's the wrong side for him, that means it's the right side for me. I could get on it right now. I wonder if he did that deliberately. He's a cunning customer, all right.

The Cunning Customer, placidly watching the young man with his hands on the bike, changed the conversation:

'Nice little place you've got here, as they say.'

Irony? A tumbledown little cottage, surrounded by turnip fields, with the noise of the traffic on the main road below roaring up to them.

Cunning Customer must have seen a sceptical look on

the face of his intended purchaser. He enlarged on his statement:

'I mean, it's not exactly *Homes and Gardens*, is it, or even Buckingham Palace? But it's a lot better than a bedsitter five floors up in the middle of that smog, isn't it?' And he jerked his head in the direction of the city a few miles away, easily identifiable by the yellowish grey haze that covered it.

'I mean, if you don't agree, what are you doing here anyway? Stands to reason. There's a lot going for a little place in the country. Be it ever so humble, and all that.'

Thomas was still holding the bicycle. He could feel the two different materials under his hands, their temperatures approximating, as the warmth from his left hand spread into the metal.

But the feel of the two is still so different – the metal hard and reliable, the leather soft and inviting, as if it really wanted me to sit on it.

'How come you're selling it so cheap? Why don't you keep it for your own use, if it's that good?'

'I can't ride it, I've already told you. I get puffed as soon as I start pedalling. I'd have to lose a few stone before I could ride one of those things now. But I've done many a mile on a bicycle, I have. Got quite a few prizes, in my time. Not quite Tour de France stuff, you know – but professional, all the same . . . But we're not here to talk about my past glories. All I mean is, I know a good bike when I see one. And this is a thoroughbred.'

'You still haven't told me why you're selling it so cheap.'

The man held up an admonitory hand:

'Don't say it, don't say it. I know exactly what's in your mind. And I'm not saying it isn't stolen. Mind you, I'm not saying it is. I just don't know. Got it from a man who owed me something. Don't know where he got it. Couldn't afford to ask questions. I had to get payment, in kind if not in cash. So there you are. Now you know as much about it as I do.'

Five-speed gear. Not bad. That would do me nicely to get to my classes. Could leave it at the Students' Union during the day.

The man asked another, apparently aimless, question:

'How do you get into town from here? Bus?'

'Yes.'

'Good bus service?'

'Not bad. Sometimes I get a lift from the farmer along the road. He's my landlord.'

Of course, I may not get any lifts from him now. Not after Norma saying I'd jilted her. Stupid boot! As if there ever had been anything serious between us. Still, I suppose he's bound to take his daughter's side in the affair. Now, if I had a bike . . .

'Must come to quite a bit, doesn't it? The fares, I mean. All those bus rides.'

Come to think of it, it would be a saving in the long run. If the bike's all right, that is.

Almost without premeditation, the right hand left the saddle and moved over to the handlebars. Then one foot on the pedal, a little extra pressure on the ground with the other foot, and we're off! Feels great!

He cycled a few yards towards the farm, then turned elegantly where the road widened a little at a gate. Good, that was, did it in style. Let's go down to the main road and see what it's like coming back up that steep bit.

Just as he was about to sail downhill he remembered about the brakes. Better test them first. Don't want to charge straight into the traffic down there.

The brakes worked so perfectly that he nearly sailed over the handlebars.

'I tell you,' chuckled the man, 'It's a good little bike. Top-notch.'

Downhill. Sailing. Glorious. 'See, bird, I fly, I fly.' Who wrote that? Can't remember. Brake now. Great!

Getting back up the hill was quite a struggle, but he made it in bottom gear.

With a bit of practice I could float right up. Well, nearly.

'Seven,' he said as he got back.

'Ten. Not a penny less. I owe it to myself. And to you. I couldn't let you cheat an innocent man like that.'

'Eight, then.'

'Nine.'

'Done!'

Thomas went into the cottage and took nine pounds out of his carefully saved money.

'Meant to pay my rent, that was,' he said ruefully as he handed it over. 'Don't know what I'm going to tell the farmer.'

'Never mind, mate. You'll think of something.'

God, I'll have to! Just after this business with Norma, too! He'll roast me, if I can't pay in full.

'Well, I'll shuffle off now.'

The man stepped over to where the bike was resting against the cottage wall, where it looked quite at home. He gave it a little pat on the saddle.

'Be seeing you.'

Which of us does he mean? Me or the bike?

Suddenly Thomas saw the man as a figure of profound pathos, as he started literally shuffling away.

'Would you like a cup of tea before you go?'

'Wouldn't say no.' The man had turned round ponderously. 'Never say no to a cuppa. That's part of the problem,' and he patted his bulging waistline.

183

The man sat back in the one armchair, with his fingers lovingly laced round the warm mug.

'I'll take two,' he said as Thomas offered him a tin with biscuits in it. 'That'll save you getting up again.'

He put down the mug and started hoisting his top half up from the armchair, to look inside the tin. Thomas spotted the eager, almost avid expression in his eyes.

He's hungry, poor devil!

'Or would you like a sandwich?'

The man paused, looking from the tin to Thomas, then back to the tin. He was evidently undecided.

'Yes,' he pronounced at last. 'Both. A sandwich and the biscuits, if you don't mind. Yes, to be perfectly frank, I should like both.'

Thomas went over to the kitchen end of the little room and started preparing a sandwich.

'It's only cheese,' he admitted. Why am I apologizing? 'Can't afford luxuries like *pâté de foie gras*.'

'Very overrated stuff, that. Grossly overrated.' The man sounded quite categorical about it. 'Nothing wrong with a good piece of . . . ' He paused to peer inside the sandwich Thomas had just handed him.

'Mousetrap, I'm afraid,' said Thomas humbly.

'Mousetrap it is. Nothing wrong with mousetrap. Lucky mice, that's what I say.'

There was a silence while the man concentrated on his sandwich, and Thomas reflected on this totally unexpected relationship he found himself involved in.

Collusion, that's what you could call it. I've bought a bike from him that I suspect may be stolen. And he either suspects it or actually knows it. But from the moment I paid him, I'm in it with him. I've got a bargain from him, I think, and we've struck a bargain between us. Tacitly, of course. He's let me have the bike at a derisory price on the

184

understanding that I don't give him away. And I've sealed the bargain by giving him food and drink. That always implies an obligation, a kind of covenant. He is now my guest. That makes it a sort of sacred tie.

Telling himself there was no need to get all poetic about it, Thomas offered the biscuit tin again, the sandwich having been consumed with evident satisfaction.

Once again the man leaned forward to examine the contents, and chose his two biscuits with the care of a connoisseur.

After another pause devoted to munching, 'Nice, seeing all these books. What you studying?'

'Philosophy and psychology.'

'Dry stuff. Drama, that was my line.'

'You mean . . . acting?'

'That's right. Shakespeare. "Now is the winter of our discontent" . . . ' He paused and took a gulp of tea.

Bet that's all he knows. The man's a charlatan.

' . . . "made glorious summer by this sun of York" . . . ' Another pause, another gulp.

He got through the whole speech in this way.

'Do you still act?'

Irony there. I think the answer to that one must be, all the time.

'Oh, not now. No. They don't want me now. "I know thee not, old man: fall to thy prayers." And they never wanted me all that much, even when I was young, to tell you the truth. I spent most of the time resting, as they say.'

'Was this before or after you took up cycling as a profession?'

A bit malicious of me, that. Why should I want to catch him out?

The man laughed, and his huge paunch heaved up and down. 'You think you've caught me out, don't you? Well, you have. And then again, you haven't. An actor has a lot of lives. And they're all true, every one of them.'

'Well—'

'You don't believe me, do you? At your age everything has to be *this* or *that*, but not both. But it *is* both, nearly always it's both.'

'You mean true and not true, fact and fiction?'

'Exactly. And fiction, young man, is the greatest truth of them all.'

Seeing a look of ironic disbelief on Thomas's face, he broke into Shakespeare again. '"There are more things in heaven and earth, Horatio—"'

'Than are dreamed of in my philosophy?' Let him see I'm not an utter ignoramus. That'll show him.

'In your philosophy and in your psychology too. Ever heard of parallel truths?'

'I'm afraid not.'

'I'm not surprised. I've just invented the term. But it's a good one. Yes, very good.'

Thomas had to admit, perhaps a bit grudgingly, that it was indeed not bad.

Wish I'd thought of it myself, in fact. Wonder if I could use that phrase in the philosophy tutorial?

The man got up and walked to the door. At the threshold he paused and raised one hand in a valedictory gesture:

'Young man, you have fed the hungry, you have welcomed the stranger within your gate, and you have listened to his ramblings with less than average disbelief and boredom . . . '

'Oh, I haven't been bored – not in the least.'

'No disclaimer, I note, in the matter of the disbelief. However, to continue: you have fed the hungry, et cetera, et cetera . . . You have sacrificed an unknown proportion of your rent, but you have gained a bicycle that shall be to you as a friend and companion. May you have many happy miles and many contented hours together. *Dixi.*'

And once again the man shuffled away. As he started going down the steep hill he turned and waved. At least, Thomas took it to be a wave, but it was more as if he were holding out his hand in blessing.

Odd character! But not boring, certainly not boring.

The following morning Thomas was waiting for the bus as usual at the main road. But this time he was on his bike, and as soon as the bus appeared he set off as fast as he could. For a few hundred yards he managed to hold his own; but the first steepish hill slowed him down, and the bus roared triumphantly past.

Well, I didn't expect to beat the bus, did I? As long as the journey doesn't take me much longer. And think of the money I'm saving!

Once he got into the outskirts of the city he was pleased to find he was making better progress than most of the cars. And just before reaching the Union he caught up with the bus, which had stopped to let off some passengers. He shot past it with a thumbs up gesture that must have surprised the driver.

Yah! he thought, as he swerved dangerously into the Union car park.

Going home in the afternoon was sheer bliss. Not having to wait forty minutes after his last class, getting away well before the rush-hour. And the feel of it.

The lovely tingle of fresh air on your skin, the delicious tinkle of the bell, the whirr of the wheels, the click when you change gear, the faint vibration of the whole machine . . . Sheer bliss.

And I'll be home long before the bus; the crowded,

smelly, stop-at-every-lamppost bus. Fancy having to pay for all that discomfort and frustration!

His euphoria subsided a bit in the evening, when he began getting nagging thoughts about the bike's ownership. At first, when he had assumed the thing had been stolen, his main concern had been the fear of having it reclaimed and losing his money. Also, he had a vague idea that you could be prosecuted for receiving stolen property.

Now, however, his thoughts turned to the moral questions involved. He thought of all the pleasure the bike was giving him, and then wondered whether somebody else was being deprived of all this. Somebody who probably had a stronger claim, having presumably paid the full price for the bike.

Whereas I got it for absurdly little. I'm not even sure that I was justified in taking it for such a sum. All right, the old chap seemed quite pleased with the deal, but still. I've got a bargain, he was quite right, I've got a real bargain. But do I have a right to it? That's the question. For a student of moral philosophy to be in this position, it's not good enough, it's really not good enough. I'll definitely have to think this one out.

Perhaps I could bring the question up in Dr Still's tutorial. The problem raises all sorts of interesting points. The whole question of property; good faith; civic duty; of paying a fair price for what you get; the innocent victim; of collusion, and turning a blind eye.

For a while he wondered whether Dr Still's tutorial was the best forum for such a discussion. These philosophers do tend to take a general view of things, to deal in abstractions. Not all that good on concrete examples, are they? Not *practical*, that's their trouble.

And here he got on to one of his habitual grouses about the course. They're so hung up on epistemology that you can't really talk about anything except whether we really have any rational grounds for talking about what we're talking about – or anything else, for that matter.

And if I say anything about the ownership of the bike they'll all stop me and say, 'What do you *mean* by "ownership"?' Definitions! That's all they can think of. Define definition, that's their favourite pastime. Till you do that you can get nowhere. So that's exactly where we do get.

Discouraged, Thomas decided to let the matter rest. After all, if he had bought a stolen bike, he didn't actually know that it was stolen, so he was in the clear. Surely? Perhaps even the old chap himself was in the clear. Perhaps he really had received it in all innocence, in settlement of a debt.

Well, innocence didn't seem to be one of his outstanding qualities, did it? Quite a character, really, an intelligent and entertaining man, but not innocent. Pathetic, rather.

Yes, pathetic, a man who has seen better days. But shrewd too. He really made a good job of selling me that bike. What you would call the soft sell, I suppose. Very unobtrusive. No pushing. But he knew what he was doing.

It was manoeuvring me into holding the bike that did it. He must have known what it would do to me, actually getting the feel of the thing. That one movement, when he tipped the bike over towards me, and I had to take hold of it to keep it from falling against me, that's what did it. And then he changed the conversation. Stopped even talking about the bicycle. Spoke about my nice little place here. Just to give me time to get the feel of the thing. He's a Cunning Customer, all right.

He knew the man had twisted him round his little finger, but it didn't matter, really. He was glad he'd got the bike. And the problem of paying the rent could be tackled by staying on late to do a couple of hours' dishwashing in the student canteen in the evenings, till he'd made up the deficit. He just didn't want to face Norma's father with an apology for not having the full rent. He could, of course, have sold the bike. Probably got a lot more for it than he'd paid.

But no, that was out of the question. He was enjoying his riding far too much. He'd even named the thing. Pegasus. A good name. It flew like a living creature beneath him, carrying him along in wind and sun and rain. And when he got to the end of the farm road in the evening, too tired to battle up the incline with all his books and notebooks in the panniers, and got off and pushed, and they tackled the hill together . . . Yes, Pegasus, Pegasus . . . He could almost feel it was alive.

No question of selling Pegasus. I'd rather work till midnight in the kitchens of Hell.

After a week he'd earned the required amount and was able to pay his rent on the right day.

Great! I'm my own man again! Back to where I was, with Pegasus for company into the bargain.

The following day he saw the man again. He was standing in front of one of the cottages at the side of the road, and he was talking to a teenage boy. Both were so engrossed in their conversation that they didn't see Thomas. And there was a bike between the man and the boy. The pose was exactly the same as Thomas had seen on that first occasion. The man was standing on the wrong side of the bike, supporting it with his left hand on the saddle and his right hand on the handlebars. The boy was looking down at the bike with an expression of the deepest interest, almost of longing.

Just as Thomas was about to pass he caught sight of the familiar movement, as the man took his hands off the bike, tipping it over gently towards the boy, whose hands stretched out to grasp it.

Just as I did. Just as I did. He's a goner, that boy. Just hope he can pay for it.

He was quite shaken by the sight of the little scene being re-enacted before him, and it brought back all his agonizing over the moral questions involved. For there could be no doubt now about the nature of the game the man was playing. Another debtor paying up in kind instead of in cash? Or the same one again? Go on!

No, there's no other possible explanation, the bikes must be stolen. How else could he get hold of them and sell them so cheap? I've been a mug. I should have known not to believe that story. And I didn't, I didn't. Not till I got my hands on you, that is. And he gave Pegasus a friendly but reproachful tap on the handlebars.

And where does that leave us? Do I go to the police and explain all about it, and tell them where I've just seen the rascal going through exactly the same routine?

And what happens then? Do I lose Pegasus? Just then he ran over an uneven piece of road surface, and Pegasus shuddered beneath him.

The worst of it, of course, would be the loss of Pegasus. But that wasn't the only problem. He didn't at all fancy going to the police with the story. He could just see their amused disbelief at his naivety, first in believing the man's story, and second in coming to them with his confession plus denunciation. They'll think I'm a real wally, won't they?

There was also the problem about his feelings for the man. There was something both likeable and pathetic about him.

Yes, likeable, and pathetic, when you think of how he's come down in the world. But there's more than that to him. He's got a great sense of how to handle people, a very fine touch. And presence, too. That final peroration, as he left. Really well handled. Who else would make a speech like that, and even finish up with *Dixi*?

And then there was the question of his obligation to the

man. They had struck a bargain, albeit an unspoken one. And he had sealed it by giving the man food and drink. Was he going to betray him now?

Thomas spent a restless night, wakening frequently and wondering where he stood, morally speaking, in the question of the bike's ownership. On the one hand, he was now convinced that his moral right to Pegasus was very tenuous indeed. On the other hand, he simply wasn't prepared to do anything that might endanger his continued ownership (or perhaps, better put, *possession*) of the bicycle.

He simply didn't know what he ought to do. If only someone would give him a clear lead! If someone else could really convince him that he had no right to Pegasus, he thought he could just manage to find it in his heart to give him up, painful as the parting, and the betrayal, would be. On the other hand, if anyone could persuade him that he was utterly innocent in his ownership, and that he had a perfect right to keep the thing . . .

If only . . .

As he cycled in to his classes next morning he came to the conclusion that the only thing that would get him out of his misery was the advice of a competent person. And who better than a moral philosopher?

I won't raise the question in the tutorial, that would be the wrong thing. He'd be bound to feel he had to answer with abstractions and prior definitions. No, I'll speak to him after the class. Man to man, that's it. Then he'll surely let me know where my duty lies.

'Dr Still, can I have a word with you?'

'Is it about the syllabus? The new list . . . '

'No, not about the syllabus. It's about Pegasus.'

'Pegasus?'

'Pegasus is my bicycle.'

192

Dr Still's face lit up. 'Really? I once had a bike called Pegasus.'

Thomas was horrified, till he remembered the bike had come to him unnamed. Couldn't possibly be the same bike.

'Many years ago, when I was a young lad studying the Classics. I hope your Pegasus is behaving well?'

'Oh, yes. Perfectly.' Thomas felt relieved. The bike had not been stolen from Dr Still, at any rate.

'Well then, what's the problem?'

'The problem is that I think it's stolen.' Thomas explained the whole history in detail, ending up with an impassioned plea for advice.

'I'll tell you exactly what you should do. By the way, what colour is the bike?'

'Blue. Dark blue. But I don't see . . .'

'Now, listen to what I'm telling you. I speak *ex cathedra*, and what I have to say is very important. What you must do is go along to the nearest shop that sells paint, and buy some bicycle paint, of any colour under the sun, except dark blue. You can't be too careful.' Dr Still beamed.

Thomas heaved a sigh of relief, and thanked him.

Rum lot, these philosophers. Can be practical after all.

He ran out to the bicycle shed and put an affectionate and thankful hand on the bike's seat.

Pegasus, we've been reprieved. Then he administered a few gentle pats to the leather, and put his books into the panniers.

He went straight to the bicycle shop and bought some paint. Black, sober black. As little eye-catching as possible, that would be the safest bet. He left the shop, determined to think no more about Pegasus' origins. And if he saw the Cunning Customer again, he would just look the other way. Forget the whole business, that's it.

The lights turned red just as he got to the busiest crossing in town. Rather than wait, he dismounted and pushed his bike along the pavement. Doesn't make you very popular, but it does save time.

Edging round the corner, trying to avoid the hurrying crowd, he found himself face to face with a similar transgressor. Both bicycles stopped dead, their front wheels more or less rubbing noses.

'Well, if it isn't my young friend!' The Cunning Customer was gazing at Thomas with evident delight.

Damn it, am I never going to get shot of him?

'Oh, hello!' Trying to sound surly. And yet pleased, in a way, to see the man again. Then, nodding towards the man's bicycle, 'Another creditor?'

'Yes, another creditor.' And the man smiled an innocent smile. Then, almost imperceptibly, he winked.

He then proceeded, 'You know, Shakespeare said, "Neither a borrower nor a lender be." But I'm not quite sure he got it right on this occasion. There's a lot to be said for a little discreet lending. But then, you can overdo it. There's the Golden Mean. We mustn't forget the Golden Mean. And that is why, my dear young friend, this is the last time we are likely to bump into each other. And I say "bump" advisedly,' he added, making his front wheel bump gently into Pegasus.

'You're leaving the area?'

'Yes, my friend, I am leaving the area. For the good of my health, as they say. Tomorrow to fresh woods . . . ?' He paused expectantly.

'And pastures new,' Thomas concluded for him.

'Exactly,' said the man. 'I knew you wouldn't let me down.'

And with that double-edged affirmation he wheeled his bicycle away from Pegasus and walked off, whistling *Land of Hope and Glory*.

22

Rag Doll

He hated the old women in their long black skirts. He hated the black, beady eyes in the dark, wrinkled face, the black kerchief tied under the chin. Like beetles, he thought, huge, black, malevolent beetles. The whole village seemed to be full of them, loitering in doorways, pushing their way through the crowd between the market stalls, standing in little groups, talking, muttering, hissing.

On a bad day he felt as if they had taken over the entire village. Droves of them filled the hot, dusty streets, coming towards him, threatening, ready to swallow him up in their long, swaying skirts.

If he saw one in the street as he left the house to go and play with his friend Joanet three doors down, he would run back and take refuge in the hall, behind one of the leaves of the great door. He would stand there, feeling the coolness of the tiled wall behind him, thinking of the thickness of the wood that was protecting him, waiting for the old witch to go past.

'Ramon, Ramonet!' His mother would pick him up and carry him through the long hallway, through the French windows of the dining-room, to the *eixida* at the back of the house. And she would stand there, holding him just a little longer, though he was really too heavy for her now. 'What is it, Ramonet?'

'*Les velles.*'

'Oh, but you mustn't mind the old women. They won't do

you any harm.'

'They're witches. *Bruixes*. And witches are wicked. You know they're wicked. It says so in all the stories.'

It was all right when he went with his mother to the market. She carried her big basket in one hand, with the white cotton bag for the bread hanging from her wrist by its draw-string. And the other hand always held Ramon's hand, and that kept the old women away.

It was when his mother stopped to buy something that he began to feel less secure, for she needed her second hand to choose the fruit and vegetables, put them into her basket, pay the stallholder.

'Senyora Pepeta, how much are your pomegranates today?'

And his mother would lift one, and then another, to see how heavy they were. For if they weren't heavy enough that meant they were too old, and had lost all their juice.

Senyora Pepeta would expatiate on the virtues and excellence of her pomegranates, and his mother would lift one rosy globe after another, weighing them in her hand. And Ramon would be looking round anxiously, knowing that the old women might gather at any moment and make a rush at him.

He knew he ought to kill the old women. Well, somebody ought to, anyway. In all the stories the old witch got killed in the end, and then they, the good people, all lived happily ever after. He had tried persuading his parents of this necessity, but they would not be swayed. Then he thought that perhaps with Joanet's help . . . But Joanet said they weren't witches at all, so there was no need to kill them.

Ramon spent a lot of the time sitting in the *eixida*, under the shade of the lemon tree. It was cool there, even on the hottest summer days, with a delicious draught blowing in all the way through the house. And he knew that the witches

196

couldn't get at him. They'd have to walk right through the house, past his mother sitting sewing in the dining-room. And she would stop them.

At night the old women came and stood beside his bed. Every night. Even though his parents left a night-light burning, they came all the same. He could see them lurking in the corners; then, one after another, they came out and stood round his bed, leaning over him, breathing over him. Old, and black, and wrinkled. Evil. Witches.

Sometimes he could stand it no longer, and screamed. And his parents came and comforted him, and held him till he fell asleep. In the morning the old women were all gone.

Sometimes he felt too ashamed to call for his parents, and lay there in an agony of fear, with his eyes tight shut, so as not to see the harpies. And, after a long, long time, he would begin to feel drowsy. The old women were still there, but there was something else too – this swaying, floating sensation, and then the words would start coming, just scraps of sentences that didn't make sense, that referred to nothing he could think of.

' . . . and that was when the apple came . . . not with the same scissors . . . catching on the climb . . . gave him ten-year marigolds . . . '

And when he woke up in the morning all the old women were gone. But he knew they were there, outside, in the street, lurking in doorways. Waiting for him.

One night the old women closed in on him so completely that he could see nothing but black all round about him and above him. He tried to scream, but no scream would come. His mouth was wide open, his throat was aching with the effort, but no sound came. He fought with his clenched fists, but the blackness was soft and moist, like treacle, and his fists simply slid about in it, unable to find anything to hit.

The old women formed a black funnel over him, shutting out everything else, sucking him in. And the funnel became a well – deep, deep, endlessly deep, and he was being pulled down, down. It was like the well in the *eixida*, which you could look into through the grille that covered it. But someone had taken the grille off, and he was falling down, down, and the well was the well, their own well, and it was also made up of the old women – dozens of them, hundreds of them, stacked one on top of another, packed so close that there was not a chink for even the tiniest ray of light to get in.

And they were all singing the song that he sang with the other children every time the sun shone through rain:

Plou i fa sol, les bruixes es pentinen
Plou i fa sol, les bruixes porten dol.

And these witches, like the ones in the song, were also combing their hair and wearing mourning. But they were always in mourning, these old women, always in black.

They must have taken the kerchiefs off their heads to be able to comb their hair. He couldn't see, it was too dark; but he knew they were combing their long, stringy hair, because he could feel it floating about, like seaweed, getting in his mouth, tangling with his hair, winding round his neck.

At last he knew he'd got to the bottom of the well, he could feel something solid beneath his feet. Solid, but not firm. It reminded him of the feeling of walking on a new-laid concrete pavement. He had rather enjoyed it at the time, till the workmen had seen him and bawled him off. Then he had tried to run, and his feet had slipped on the wet cement, and he had nearly fallen, and thought one of the workmen was going to catch him.

This time he couldn't even try to run, for there was this wall of witches all round him, hemming him in.

At last he felt as if the old women were receding. And then the swaying, floating feeling came, and the disjointed bits of sentences.

. . . forked in tender drill . . . the song sang its something . . . country from the across fan . . .

Sinking, sinking . . .

And he was standing alone in the darkness, and he could sense that it extended for miles round about him, and he was standing there alone, sinking, sinking . . .

They found the old doll when they were clearing out the attic. It must have been very old, the kind called a *pepa de ral*, a sort of sixpenny rag doll. Its clothes were grey with dust, almost black.

'I wonder what little girl played with that, all those years ago?' said his mother. 'She must be an old, old woman by now.'

Later on Ramonet found the old doll on top of the dustbin, waiting to be thrown out. Looking round warily to make sure he wasn't observed, he summoned all his courage and picked the doll up delicately, holding it by the skirts, between forefinger and thumb, reluctant to come into contact with it. It had cost him a big effort to decide to put his plan into action, because of the fear and disgust that this doll inspired in him – this doll that had belonged to one of the old women, and looked rather like one of them herself, in her blackened clothes.

He stepped out of the kitchen into the *eixida*, still holding the doll fastidiously by her skirts. Crossing over to the well he looked at the size of the spaces in the grille. It was just as he had feared – not nearly big enough to get the doll through. And yet, he must, he must. This was his one chance.

He looked back again towards the house. Nobody.

Then, gritting his teeth, he took hold of the head in one hand and one of the arms in the other, and pulled. To his surprise, the doll offered little resistance. Almost at once he found himself with a dismembered arm in one hand, while a little sawdust trickled out on to the tiled area round the well.

He had no difficulty in popping the arm through the grating into the well. He then pulled off the other one and did the same with it. Then he held the amputated doll above the grille, to see if it would now go through the space available. Yes; the head went through, even the shoulders, with a little pressure.

He was just about to let go when he pulled the truncated body back up again. With a sudden surge of fury he pulled the head right off, then stuffed both head and body through the grating. In a few seconds he heard a faint sound, something between a plop and a splash.

Before leaving the well he turned his attention to the three little piles of sawdust that lay on the tiles. With his foot he edged them over to the sandy soil of the nearest flower bed. Then he ground them hard into the dry soil.

That was the end of the doll, the end of the witches. The old women would never trouble him again.

23

Wild Wattie

He was a wild boy. Even as a child they thought he was wild. Wild Wattie, they called him.

He knew from the start that school was not for him, and he defied them all – father, mother, teacher, friends and relations. And he won in the end. Most days instead of going to school he would be up the hill on his own, running with the foxes, listening to the burn, perched high up in the branches of a tree, talking to the birds.

He felt a great indifference for all the domestic animals, an indifference that bordered on contempt.

They weren't proper animals at all. They'd chosen to be prisoners.

Repeatedly he tried to give them their freedom. He opened gates, he untied halters. He even let the bull out, to wander through the lanes till it got to the village, where it was captured and returned to the unsuspecting farmer. That earned Wattie a terrible beating, for the whole village was up in arms. He never did that again, not so much because of the severity of the beating, as because of his disgust at the docility with which the enormous beast had allowed itself to be led home. This kingly creature was a slave at heart, it seemed.

He's not right in the head. The best thing is to leave him alone. He's wild. Yes, he's wild, but he's not stupid. God, no, he's not stupid. He gets what he wants, doesn't he? Best leave him alone. He could be dangerous.

Wattie knew what people thought of him. He didn't care. If the others had known what he thought of them they would have understood why he didn't care.

His mother died when he was ten years old. Grief, that's what it was, grief and worry over this wild son of hers. His brothers were afraid of him, even the eldest, two years older than Wattie. His father virtually ignored him. He gave him food and shelter and clothing. Nothing else. No conversation, no scoldings or beatings or caring. No love.

It was hard to love Wattie, and nobody succeeded. His mother had tried very hard, his father too, at first. And the teacher, an old-fashioned Scottish dominie, had done his best to tame this wild creature. But he too had failed. Wattie seemed to feel for mankind the same scorn that he felt for the animals they had domesticated. They had all forsworn the freedom to which they were born.

By the time he was old enough to leave school he hadn't crossed its threshold in years. And no one even suggested he should look for work.

Who's going to employ a boy like that? Never done a stroke in his life. Wouldn't know where to start. Probably do more harm than good, anyway. Remember how he emptied all the milk cans into the drain? And herded the sheep so far up the hill that they thought they'd never get them back? And the bull! Remember how he let out the bull? He's a wild, wild boy. Never talks to anyone. Hasn't for years. I think he must have lost the power of speech, by now.

But Wattie talked all right, when he was out alone in his own world. He talked to the birds and the trees and the small furry things that scuttled about him. He had plenty to say to them. He wanted to be one of them, he was one of them.

His love for the natural world was balanced by his hatred of whoever oppressed or exploited it. If he saw a man fishing he would shout and throw stones into the river to disturb the fish; he had risked his life in defence of the hunted fox; he had broken up shooting parties and been beaten for his pains. More than the loss of their game, what had outraged the sportsmen had been the word '*Cowards!*' hurled at them by this passionate young adversary.

He had no objection to eating the flesh of captive animals. These had given up their glory. The sheep and the pigs and the cattle belonged to the world of man. Corrupt. Degraded. Fallen from grace. They had traded in their freedom, for security and a full belly. They had chosen a diminished life and an ignoble death.

As a young child he had been greatly disturbed by the sight of some crows feeding on a dead rabbit. The crows and the rabbit belonged to the same world, the world of the free – the one should not prey upon the other. It shocked his sense of solidarity. But as he grew older, and realized the true relationship between the eater and the eaten, the stark law that survival for some species depends entirely on the success with which they can prey on others, he came to regard the crows and other carrion creatures as more highly evolved than the predators. At least they were not responsible for the death of the animal they feasted on.

Death was never far from his thoughts. He heard it and saw it in its various manifestations every day. From the scream of the captured rabbit to the whitened bones of a dead sheep, the ubiquitous presence of death was with him. But life was with him too, just as insistently, just as triumphantly.

He came to accept both, with serenity and curiosity. If life was continually offering him all kinds of joys and wonders, death's voice was sweet too, and infinitely mysterious. Death was the end of life, and the continuation of life, and the two were inextricably bound together.

He learned how to be still. Silent and motionless as a rock, as if rehearsing his death. He would sit for hours without moving, leaning against a tree trunk, at one with the rising sap, while the rabbits came and went from the burrow beside him, hopping over his feet as if these were only an extension of the tree. Or he would lie by the side of the burn, with his hand in the water, enjoying its chilly caress, while he watched the clouds above him, waiting for the first drop of rain to fall.

He loved the sun and he loved the rain, and the soft, mesmeric movement of the snow. But most of all he loved the wind. He loved the wind as other men love a woman. And up in the hills the beloved was never far from him. Some days it was no more than a cool, insistent breeze, reminding him of its eternal presence; but often it was a strong, masterful wind, tugging at his hair and his clothes, whistling past him, fighting him off and forcing him onwards by turns. The wind was his friend and his enemy, his master and his lover.

The happiest day of his life was the day of the Great Wind. It came howling down the valley, over the crest of the hills, tearing up trees, knocking down walls, peeling the roofs off houses as if they were so many sweet papers. There was devastation in the village, and neighbourliness reached an unwonted pitch, as the terrified people sheltered in what-ever houses seemed likeliest to withstand the onslaught.

Wattie took the storm at its height up on the hill. He was in a patch of mixed woodland not far above the village when he realized this was going to be no ordinary storm. The noise was deafening, and branches were crashing down all round about him. One of them nearly knocked him down, and made a gash in his cheek. He hardly noticed the injury, though the scar was to remain with him for the rest of his life. There was only one thought in his mind – to get up to the summit of the hill while the storm was still raging.

He struggled on in the teeth of the wind, as if he were fighting for his life – for his death, perhaps? – and at last he made it to the summit. There it was impossible to stand. He crawled about on hands and knees, looking into the hurricane, hardly able to breathe, hardly able to see for the tears that the wind kept whipping into his eyes.

Then he turned and began the descent. He followed the direction of the wind, obliquely down the hill. He ran, he almost floated, he leapt over rocks and across streams; and he howled with the wind, in an ecstasy of violence.

When he came to the place from which he could see the village he had the unspeakable joy of seeing one of the roofs lifting off and travelling over the next two houses before it was blown into the side of the church, where it shattered like a broken tile.

Suddenly Wattie started running again. His father's house, on the outskirts of the village, was in an open, windy spot. It had struck him their roof too might be blown off, and he wanted to be there when it happened. In his overexcited state nothing seemed too big a price to pay for such a spectacle.

The roof survived, and soon the storm had blown itself out. Till nightfall he wandered about, looking at the wreckage, feeding on the results of the violence that had so uplifted him.

He never quite got over this experience, and spent the rest of his life longing for a return of the wild joy he had felt as he had rushed down the hill, howling with the wind. For some moments he had no longer been himself. He had given himself to the wind, and the wind had taken him and filled him with its own boundless power and joy. And he longed to be transported again in this way.

Perhaps it was this storm that had damaged the branch he was on some months later, when it suddenly gave way under him. He heard the crack and felt the branch yielding beneath his weight. He was too high up to hope to land safely on his feet, and threw himself forward on to another branch. But it snapped like a matchstick under his weight. He fell heavily to the ground, and rolled a few yards down the hill, into a little clearing.

His right ankle and thigh were both causing him the most excruciating pain. He knew right away that there was no question of his being able to walk. He would have to lie here till he was found or till he died of exposure.

He had plenty of time to think over his two possibilities. Being rescued would mean weeks, perhaps months, captive in hospital. And after that? What guarantee that he would ever be able to walk again? For the first time he realized that his whole way of life depended on his ability to come and go as he pleased, to climb and to run, to put as many miles as he wished between himself and other people, to be surrounded by rocks and trees instead of bricks and mortar. To have the company of birds and animals and insects instead of the irritating, insensitive presence of his fellow men. No, the thought of surviving maimed, necessarily tamed, filled him with dread.

As for the other option . . . He was determined to consider it an option, for he was miles from the village, in a wild area where no other man ever came in winter. Even if they sent out a search party – and would they? – hidden as he was in the wood it was most unlikely that they would actually find him unless he called out. So the choice was virtually his. Provided he kept quiet, even if he heard them calling him, he could have his solitary death. He would be able to avoid the misery of a domesticated shadow of life.

How long would it take, he wondered. It was bitterly cold, snow was threatening. He suspected that death from exposure might come quite quickly.

He lay there thinking of his longing for another transport-ing experience like the ecstasy the hurricane had brought him. Death, perhaps? What would it be like? Would he know when it was approaching? Passionately he wanted to know. He didn't want to miss his death. The animals knew, he felt sure. They lay down and waited, ready to savour their death to the full. It seemed to him that he was being given the chance to die like the wild creatures. How much better to die like this than in hospital, doped and drugged and blunted out of all knowledge of the supreme moment! He would not be cheated out of the final answer.

Where's Wattie? Did he not come home last night?
No, haven't seen him since yesterday morning.
That's odd. I wonder what he's up to.
I shouldn't worry. He often stays out all night.
Not in this weather. You'd die of exposure, out all night when it's this cold.
I shouldn't worry. He knows how to take care of himself.

Two days later he heard them calling him. They were quite far away, and there was no danger they would see him, unless they came much nearer. He lay still, silent. Stillness came easily to him. He had spent so much time keeping still, while the sparrows taught their young to fly at his feet, watching an insect crawling over his hand, waiting to see if the wildcat he had glimpsed would come out again and make friends with him. As he lay there he thought about the fact that its lair was quite near here. Perhaps it would come now. He was lying so very still.

The stillness helped him to endure the pain. The cold helped too. Eventually he became so numb that he hardly felt anything at all.

Later it began to snow, and he watched, entranced, as the

flakes fell tenderly and silently. It made him sleepy to watch them. Some fell into his eyes and he kept having to blink them away. After a while the trees turned white, and he realized he too must be covered with snow, for he lay in the little clearing, with nothing but the soft grey sky above him. He felt himself drifting off into sleep. In his dream the wildcat came padding softly up to him. It stood very close, sniffing. It came closer, and closer, till he could feel the warmth of its breath on his face.

They found him the next day, dead, under a blanket of snow. They were a bit puzzled by the paw marks in the snow beside the body. A fox? No, never a fox. In the end they decided it must be a wildcat.

Yes, that was it.

A wildcat.

24

A Mob of One

From the kitchen Conxa could hear the wailing coming up the stair well. She sighed. Pepito again, no doubt. As the howling came closer she recognized the familiar mixture of desolation and outrage. Yes, Pepito all right.

Pepito was really giving it all he'd got, this time. So much so that, on various levels of the tenement, doors were opened, and exclamations of dismay could be heard.

Conxa opened the door of the flat just as the howling reached maximum intensity. Pepito, escorted by one of his friends, had just arrived on the landing.

'*Mare de Déu, què t'ha passat?*'

Pepito was too busy howling to answer.

Jaumet replied:

'He fell.'

Normally this answer would have produced a snort of disbelief in Pepito's mother. But the sight of her son's blood-stained face was enough to make her forget about the rights and wrongs of the case. She took her youngest son by the arm and guided him into the kitchen.

Filling a bowl with clean water, she started bathing the wound – a huge gash that ran diagonally across one side of the forehead, and which continued to bleed profusely.

Pepito was still screaming. In fact, he had every intention of going on screaming for some time to come. He knew he would be in deep trouble once the truth got out, and had learned that there's nothing like a good howling match for putting off retribution.

Jaumet was watching with interest.

'Quite a cut, isn't it?' he remarked appreciatively.

'How did he get it? You don't get a cut like that from a fall.'

Jaumet had his answer ready:

'He tripped and fell and hit his head on the edge of the kerb.'

This was the answer they had all agreed on during a momentary interruption in the howling, as the boys escorted Pepito home.

'You should have seen the blood,' went on Jaumet.

'I *do* see it,' snapped the victim's mother.

'All along the street,' pursued Jaumet with fruition. 'And on the stairs.'

Conxa sighed again, but said nothing. The cut was so serious that it looked as if it should really have medical attention.

It was not unusual for Pepito to come home in a somewhat damaged state. He was a wilful and unruly child, and his parents found it hard to make him accept discipline.

'I think it's going to need stitching,' she said gloomily, as she examined the wound.

Pepito voiced his disagreement by redoubling his vocal efforts, which had abated slightly.

'Well, we'll wait till your father comes home, and see what he says. If it has stopped bleeding by that time . . . '

It had been a splendid fight.

Pepito's gang, *Els Salvatges*, had met their most fearsome rivals, *Els Tigres* in an epic battle. The engagement had been arranged beforehand by emissaries from both sides. *Els Salvatges* had been particularly keen for the encounter to take place, as three of their most active members had recently acquired new slings. In the early years of this century one of the chief forms of entertainment among the boys in the working-class districts of Barcelona was for one gang to challenge another to battle in this time-honoured mode. It was a beautifully democratic custom, for those who didn't have a sling were encouraged to join in, simply throwing stones by hand.

Pepito, who was only eight and therefore one of the younger members of the gang, had not so far risen to the ranks of the sling owners. But his enthusiasm, his speed, and his courage in rushing out from behind the defences to retrieve any enemy stones that had missed their mark, made him an invaluable member of the gang. It was as he set out on one of these forays that he had received his wound.

The battles between *Els Salvatges* and *Els Tigres* usually took place in the *Plaça del Born*, the square which housed the central fruit and vegetable market of the city. It was an ideal venue for this purpose, as there were always piles of crates and boxes which could act as barricades. And if the supply of stones happened to run short, the contestants were not above seizing the odd rotten orange or apple to act as an impromptu missile.

Serious as was the injury Pepito had sustained, it did not prevent him from rejoining the fray after his comrades had dragged him back to their own line of defence. Squinting out of his left eye, since the right one had too much blood flowing over it to see out of, he continued the attack till the enemy were routed.

It was only then that he began to feel the pain of his wound in all its intensity, and his elation quickly turned to misery and apprehension. For an injury of this magnitude could not be hidden. His parents would almost certainly find out that he had been fighting again, and this was strictly forbidden.

But Pepito, the baby of the family, was intelligent, active, and always ready for anything in the way of excitement, so the appeal of a fight, however illegal, was more than he could resist. His membership of *Els Salvatges* had already cost him several thrashings; but these had proved ineffective in making him renounce the joys of street violence.

So now he sat on the little terrace at the back of the flat waiting for his father's return with mixed feelings. Even the pain of his present injury, even the fear of being taken to the doctor for stitching, even his apprehension about his father's reaction, were not quite enough to dampen the glow of satisfaction he felt when he thought of the glorious victory he and his comrades had achieved. His parents would almost certainly find out about the fight, and would probably punish him for his disobedience – unless, of course, they might be persuaded to take the reasonable attitude that his injury was punishment enough.

When Antoni Roca came home he examined his son's injury and decided they needn't face the drama of taking him to the doctor, as the bleeding had stopped.

'What happened, anyway?' he asked.

'I fell.'

A snort from Conxa.

Antoni received the information with an urbane smile.

'Quite a coincidence, isn't it?' he said. 'There seems to have been quite a lot of bloodshed about, this afternoon. The shopkeeper at the corner told me there was a great battle between *Els Salvatges* and *Els Tigres*. It seems that *Els Salvatges* were beaten hollow.'

'We were not! We won!'

Even before his parents had burst out laughing Pepito realized his mistake.

'Well, Conxa, what do you think we ought to do with this little savage? He's been fighting again and telling lies about it.'

Conxa shook her head. 'I don't know. You're his father. It's up to you.'

'Right, Pepito,' said Antoni. 'You've had quite a nasty injury. Let that be the first part of your punishment.'

'And the second?'

'The second is that you'll have a scar on your forehead for the rest of your life.'

As if I cared, thought Pepito. In fact, an honourable scar was something to be proud of. His spirits had just about reached their normal high level, when his father spoke again.

'*And,* one other thing. Next time, I go straight to school and tell your teachers.'

Pepito was terrified of the teachers in his school. They were all priests, and had the reputation of being very severe. He feared and hated them all, and thought of them as black, malevolent cockroaches. And the worst of it was that Pepito was a bright boy, anxious to learn, but so in dread of his teachers that school had become a purgatory to him, and he had lost all interest in the work.

'You wouldn't tell them at school would you?'

'Yes, I would. So don't let me hear of any more of these street fights, or you know what will happen.' His father spoke quite sternly this time.

Pepito knew he meant what he said. His fear of being reported to the priests was not quite enough to make him decide on future obedience – after all, he had his duty to his friends, quite apart from his natural inclination. But he went to bed that night with the conviction that life was a more solemn business than he had realized. He would continue to play his part in *Els Salvatges*;

but he now saw that the price of discovery would be great indeed.

Pepito's dread of the priests was something that was to stay with him all his life, and coloured his reaction to the terrible events of the *Setmana Tràgica*. In 1909, as a result of popular protest against massive conscription for what the people considered an incomprehensible and alien war in Morocco, riots broke out in Barcelona, a general strike was declared and barricades were set up in the streets. By the end of that tragic week there were more than a hundred dead, among them three priests, and hundreds of wounded. As had happened before and has happened since in Barcelona, the unrest took on a strongly anticlerical form. On this occasion as many as half the churches and other religious buildings in the city were destroyed.

By now Pepito was thirteen years old. In spite of his fear and hatred of the priests he had learned to take an interest in his studies, and this had had a civilizing effect on him. He no longer belonged to *Els Salvatges*, and would never have dreamed of picking up even the most attractive stone to use as a weapon.

His desire for independence had now taken an intellectual rather than a bellicose turn.

But when the violence broke out in the streets he felt a thrill run through him, and longed to take his share in it, the more so because of the anticlerical nature of the rising. His new-found conviction, strengthened by the beliefs of his parents, that this was a barbarous way to behave, was badly shaken by the exciting rumours that were circulating all the time – churches burned, convents sacked, the bodies of nuns exhumed and paraded through the streets. It was wrong, he knew it was wrong; but still, he would have given anything to witness the violence, perhaps even take part in it.

214

Aware of the temptation that this state of affairs meant for Pepito, his parents forbade him to leave the house.

Pepito was outraged:

'But I've got to go to school!'

'Not while this is going on.'

'But I'll get into trouble if I don't go. The priests will beat me.'

'It might be the priests who get the beating for once. And that's precisely why you're not going near the place. Right now a school is one of the most dangerous places you could be. They might set your one on fire. It wouldn't be the first.'

His father's words had a quite unintended effect on Pepito – inflammatory rather than pacific. From that moment onwards he was in a fever of excitement and frustration. The thought that the hated building might be attacked, even destroyed, when he wasn't there to see it, was more than he could bear. He tried to settle down to studying his French and Latin, but even his beloved languages failed to erase the gorgeous vision of the school with flames leaping out of its windows, and all the priests running for their lives, with their skirts tucked up and their hats flying.

Towards the end of the week he could stand it no longer. After his mother had gone out to do the shopping he waited for a minute or two, then slipped out, ran down the stairs, and paused at the street door, to make sure his mother wasn't in sight. He knew she was only going to the two nearest shops, so as to spend as little time as possible in the streets.

He was just in time to see her go into one of the shops a little way along the street. He stepped out and ran off in the opposite direction. She would find out, of course. In a few minutes she would be back, and would immediately check to see he was still sitting in the dining-room with his books spread out on the table. The books would be there all right, but no reader. Pepito chuckled as he thought of his mother's surprise and fury. He would pay for it, he knew. But it wouldn't be his first thrashing. And how could they expect him to miss an historic occasion like this?

The streets were very quiet, almost awesomely quiet. He made straight for the school, hoping to find it ablaze. But the huge, grim building seemed exactly as usual, only strangely silent. Instead of the conflicting chants of childish voices intoning verbs, catechism, multiplication tables in a weary sing-song, a sinister hush had settled on the place. He wondered whether the priests had barricaded themselves inside.

Reluctantly, he gave up hope of watching the disintegration of the abhorred seat of learning, and set off in search of action.

Nor did it take him long to find it.

As he turned into one of the narrow streets near the school he met a crowd coming towards him, shouting in a disorganized manner. He couldn't make out much of what they were saying, but understood that they were looking for one of the priests from the nearby church.

Just as the mob came to the part of the street Pepito was in they stopped, and those in front went through the doorway of one of the tenement flats and began climbing the stairs. Soon Pepito was completely surrounded by the crowd, who were all milling about, waiting for their companions to come back with the priest.

Pepito wasn't tall for his age, and couldn't see above the heads of the crowd, so he backed into a doorway opposite the one under attack, and stood on a large wooden box that had been left there. This gave him a splendid view of the proceedings. It also made him feel rather safer. He was afraid that, if he lost his footing in the mob he would be trampled underfoot.

For a few minutes nothing happened, and the crowd seemed to get angrier and angrier. In among the shouting Pepito could hear a few hysterical screams and some uncontrolled laughter. It was exciting, certainly, but he was beginning to discover that he didn't really like being there in the middle of this disturbing sense of imminent violence.

At last a window was flung open three floors up, and a man appeared shouting, '*Ja el tenim!*'

So, they'd got him. A cheer went up from the mob, which surged even more closely round the doorway through which the captive priest was to appear.

After another minute or two, people started coming out of the house; among them the tall figure of a priest. He was being pushed from one to another of the mob, handled roughly, shouted at with the accumulated hatred of many years. And as he was being bundled about, pushed in one direction and then in another, Pepito saw that the tonsured head had a great gash in the shaven part, from which blood was flowing freely. Mechanically he put his hand up to his own forehead, to feel the scar of his earlier exploit. He knew what it felt like, to have a cut like that.

Suddenly it seemed to him that this wasn't the same thing at all, that this wasn't playing fair. In their gang-land fights numbers had at least been relatively even, and you fought because you wanted to, by mutual agreement. But all these people against this one man? All right, the man was a priest, and he hated priests – but still!

The sense of objective justice was suddenly born in Pepito, and he felt himself more mature and more reasonable than all these adults shouting and swearing in front of him.

The priest was being pushed about, struck, spat on. Several times he lost his balance and would have fallen if the crowd hadn't pressed so closely round him. At last the man did fall, and Pepito lost sight of him.

He could bear it no longer. Somehow he managed to push his way through to the edge of the crowd, and ran for home.

Pepito knew he'd be in trouble when he got there, terrible trouble. But that didn't seem to matter too much. He'd got a much more serious problem than that to solve – the problem of right and wrong, of justice and injustice, and of why, hating priests as he did, his whole being had revolted at the way the mob was treating this one.

His mother was too thankful to see him back in the house safe and sound to do more than refer the matter to her husband.

'He'll deal with you,' she said.

Since the truth was out and he had nothing to gain from hiding his unauthorized excursion, Pepito told his mother what he had seen, without making any mention of the tumult of thoughts and questions that the experience had evoked.

When his father came home in the evening Conxa told him where their son had been.

'Tell your father what you saw.'

Pepito told him, then asked:

'Father, it's not right, is it? It's not right to behave like that, not even to a priest?'

'No, Pepito, it's not right. Mob rule is never right, no matter what the provocation. And no matter what the size of the mob. Even if it's only a mob of one.'

'A mob of one? There's no such thing!'

'Oh, yes there is. I'm looking at one right now.'

'Me?' Pepito asked, astonished.

'Yes, you. Can you tell me why?'

Pepito thought hard for a moment. Then he said rather

sheepishly, 'Because I took the law into my own hands and went out without permission?'

His father nodded gravely. 'A mob of one is less danger-ous than a mob of hundreds. But it's every bit as wrong. Remember that.'

Pepito nodded and went out on to the balcony to look at the deserted street. He'd never had so much to think about in his life before. And of all that had happened that eventful day he felt the most important thing to remain with him would be fear and distrust of the mob.

Even a mob of one.

25

The Thimble

'Thimble? What thimble?'

'Mother's thimble, of course.'

'I don't see what's so of course about it.'

'Jack, I wish you wouldn't talk rubbish.'

'I'm not talking rubbish.'

'Yes you are. You can't say "what's so of course". That just isn't English.'

'Don't carp. You know perfectly well what I mean. And anyway, what's all this about Mother's thimble – since that appears to be the only possible thimble under discussion?'

'I don't see why it should turn into a discussion at all.'

'I didn't say it had. The term "under discussion" doesn't imply an argument.'

'You'd be surprised how often it does, where you're concerned.'

'Jessie, I am not an argumentative man. You can ask any of my friends or colleagues.'

'And I am not an argumentative woman. You can ask any of my friends or colleagues.'

They glowered at each other for a moment then, both together, suddenly burst out laughing.

'I don't know what I've done to deserve such an argumentative brother.'

'Probably much the same as I've done to deserve such a contentious sister. I expect it's hereditary.'

'We must have got it from Father, then. Mother wasn't

like that. And that reminds me, we were talking about the thimble.'

'You were, you mean.'

'Well, so were you.'

'I consider that an overstatement. I am not, as a general rule, given to talking about thimbles. In fact, I think I could truthfully state that I have never in my life felt the urge to discuss anything of the sort. It's not exactly a masculine subject, you must admit.'

'I shall refrain from calling you a male chauvinist pig.'

'Most kind of you.'

'It's not kindness. I just happen to have a fastidious dislike of stating the obvious.'

'Right, Jess, I see we're not going to get anywhere till we've had a thorough discussion of your chosen subject. So, what's it to be? With what aspect do we start? The size, shape, colour, texture, material or value of the thimble in question?'

'The location. What happened to it? That's all I want to know.'

'And what could be easier to ascertain? After all, it's only thirty years since Mother died. And we have both lived on in this house ever since. It's inconceivable that either of us should have any doubts as to the whereabouts of the object in question.'

'Jack, will you stop being flippant about it? I really want to know where that thimble is.'

'But why? Why after thirty thimbleless years is it suddenly so important to you? Why today, precisely?'

'Do you know what day it is today?'

'Nineteenth of . . . Oh, I see! This is the anniversary of her death, isn't it?'

'Thirty years to the day. And I was thinking of Mother, seeing her sitting there, by the fire, sewing, as she used to do every evening. And, I don't know why, I decided I'd look through her sewing things. And I went to her old workbox, and opened it. And I found all sorts of treasures – her little scissors, her two pincushions, one for pins and one for needles—'

'A needle-cushion, then.'

'Yes, a needle-cushion, to be exact – that was the one I made her when I was a child, and so she still kept it, even though it was looking pretty shabby. But that was like her, wasn't it?'

'Sentimental, you mean?'

'I suppose that's what a man would call it. These little things don't mean so much to you, do they? And, talking about little things, I suddenly remembered her thimble, and it wasn't there. And I can't think what can have happened to it.'

'Well, perhaps she had lost it.'

'Don't be silly, Jack. You know she was sewing the very day she died. She must have had it then.'

'Is it impossible to sew without a thimble?'

'It would be very difficult, and rather inefficient. A good needlewoman like Mother would never sew without a thimble.'

'So, what are we to do about it? Call in Scotland Yard?'

'Hardly. I expect I'm the only person in the world for whom it has any value.'

'Well, you've spent thirty years without ever thinking of it, so it can't be all that valuable even to you, can it?'

Jessie considered the matter for a moment. 'I don't know. Now that I have thought of it, suddenly it does seem very important. I'd give a lot to find it.'

'You consider the thimble a quintessential part of Mother, as it were?'

'Yes, I think I do. The thimble is a symbol of domesticity,

of industriousness – yes, I know that's a horrible word, but nothing else will do.'

Jack nodded his acquiescence. 'I accept industriousness. Go on.'

'It's a symbol of service, and love, and caring. All the things Mother used to do for us. All the old-fashioned virtues, in fact.'

'I see what you mean. If I could draw I'd paint a picture of the thimble as a cornucopia, with all these virtues spilling out of it.'

'No doubt you'd manage the thimble all right – if you could draw, that is. I'd be interested to see how you represented the virtues.'

'I suppose I'd have to fall back on a collection of well fleshed allegorical ladies with scrolls wrapped round them with their names on them.'

'Rather a lot to get into a thimble, don't you think?'

'You're just making things difficult for me. Out of sheer malice. You're not your mother's daughter at all.'

'I'm not malicious. You know I'm not.

'I was only joking.'

'I accept your apology. But I do agree. I'm not my mother's daughter in some ways. I don't have her sweetness, or her gentleness. I wish I had.'

'On the other hand . . . '

'Yes?'

'Oh, I don't know. You don't have all Mother's qualities, but you'll do.'

Jessie knew that was as near to a compliment as she would ever get from her brother, and refrained from mentioning the thimble again.

But for the rest of the evening Jack kept thinking about it. When it was time for bed he shut himself up in his room and sat down at his desk by the window. Taking the keys out of his pocket he held them in his hand for a moment, as if lost in thought. Then he unlocked the desk and opened one of its drawers. From it he took out a small object wrapped in a white handkerchief. He unwrapped the thimble and carefully smoothed out the handkerchief. Then he placed the thimble on it, right in the centre.

After a while he took a writing pad out of the desk and began writing.

Dear Jessie,

Thirty years is a long time to keep a secret. And it's a long time to keep a thimble. The day after Mother died I took it. I wanted to have something of hers to keep; and, like you, I saw it as a symbol of all the domestic and family virtues that she possessed so abundantly. It was, as we agreed, the quintessence of Mother. I knew it was selfish of me to take it; but I hoped you just wouldn't notice. And for thirty years you didn't.

I haven't forgotten that tomorrow is your birthday. As usual I've been wondering what on earth to give you. Now I know.

If we're still alive in another thirty years you can let me have it back. Or perhaps we can share it then.

Have a Happy Birthday!

Love,

Jack.

He gave a little sigh; half satisfaction, half regret. Then he carefully wrapped the thimble up in the handkerchief and popped it into the envelope beside the letter.